DEATH
AT
INISHMORE
CASTLE

BOOKS BY LUCY CONNELLY

DEATH
AT
INISHMORE
CASTLE

Lucy Connelly

bookouture

Published by Bookouture in 2025

An imprint of Storyfire Ltd.
Carmelite House
50 Victoria Embankment
London EC4Y 0DZ

www.bookouture.com

The authorised representative in the EEA is Hachette Ireland
8 Castlecourt Centre
Dublin 15 D15 XTP3
Ireland
(email: info@hbgi.ie)

ISBN: 978-1-83525-721-0
eBook ISBN: 978-1-83525-720-3

This book is dedicated to my grandchildren, who make me want the world to be a better place. So, I created this one for all of us to share.

ONE

As we pulled into the long, stone driveway of Inishmore Castle, rain pelted the car so hard that it was difficult to make out the outline of the massive stone building. The weather in Ireland in late winter was wet. Even though it was nearing noon, it was dark outside. Thunder boomed, and my sister Lizzie and I jumped.

There was a quaint wooden bridge ahead, but water from the river was already lapping over the sides. While we were only fifteen miles away from Shamrock Cove, it felt like we were in another world. This bridge was the only way into the castle grounds. From the small bit of research I'd done, that was by design so that marauders back in the day could not cross easily.

"Is it safe?" Lizzie asked.

Lightning crackled down to the earth. The vibration shook the car.

I put my foot on the gas and raced over the wooden slats, praying we wouldn't be swept away.

Once we were across, we let out a collective breath. Lightning hit the ground again, and we both yelped.

"Do you think that's a sign, Mercy?"

I laughed. "That we need to get in from this weather, yes."

Mr. Poe, our little ball of black fluff, barked from the back seat as if he agreed. I sometimes wondered if he wasn't part human. He was so in tune with our moods and seemed to understand everything we said.

My sister and some of our neighbors who sat on the local tourism committee had been invited to a weekend at Inishmore Castle, which had recently opened a whiskey-tasting tour, along with an assorted list of craft and cooking classes on the estate.

It was a dream weekend for my sister. She loved everything to do with crafts.

When it came to me, it was a chance to get away from the blank pages I'd been staring at for the last week and a half. It wasn't so much writer's block with the new novel. It was the discovery that my story wasn't working as well as it could and knowing I had so much rewriting to do.

When Lizzie asked if I wanted to tag along, I couldn't resist. I loved all things whiskey. The history of the castle was of great interest to me, as well. Places like this sparked my creativity. I wrote contemporary detective stories, but unblocking my creative brain could come from any source. My hope was after a relaxing weekend, I'd be ready to tackle my book head on.

At the very least, getting away from my computer and office for a few days wasn't a bad idea. I'd been mainlining caffeine and staring out the window into our beautiful, winter flowering garden for the last week.

The castle came into view and we both gasped. It looked like something out of one of those old gothic novels. It was at least a half of a block long and built with a beautiful stone that had weathered well with age. The land around it was lush and green, which wasn't surprising here in Ireland since it rained all the time.

"It looks like a fairy-tale castle," Lizzie said.

"Well, maybe a darker one," I added. "Look at those gargoyles. I don't think I've seen so many in one place." There were at least ten we could see, and each one appeared as if it might take flight any minute and attack us.

"Sinister for sure," Lizzie said. Then she shivered in her pink sweater set. Her hair was piled on her head in a messy bun. While my twin's hair was black, I'd recently lightened mine to a strawberry blonde. Her skin was olive, and mine burned in the sun after only a few minutes. We were the same height, but that was about it.

My sister was fond of color in her clothing, I was the opposite. My uniform was almost always black on black. It was easier to get dressed in the morning.

"It looks so much bigger than it did in the brochures," she said.

She was right.

After pulling up under the portico leading to the front door, I turned off the car. "I'll get the bags. You grab Mr. Poe," I said.

We were grateful the castle was dog-friendly and that we were able to bring him with us. Actually, I would have stayed home with him, as I couldn't imagine leaving him at a kennel for four days. We'd only had the little black dog with white fur on his chest for a few months, and he was already a third member of the family.

He was used to going everywhere with us and had become Lizzie's emotional support animal. Mine, too, if I were honest.

The portico kept us from getting even wetter, even though the rain was coming in sideways. Lizzie used the lion-faced knocker on the heavy wooden doors to announce us. A few seconds later, the door creaked open, but no one was there.

"Well, that's not creepy at all," I whispered.

We glanced at one another and stepped inside.

"You made it," Rob, our next-door neighbor, said from behind the door.

Not realizing he was there, we jumped again.

"Sorry, I didn't mean to scare you. This door is heavy, and if you don't hold it open, it shuts on its own. Scott and I found out the hard way," he said.

"Welcome to Inishmore," said a woman coming down the stairs. She was dressed in jeans, a fluffy sweater, and high leather boots. Her white hair was in a knot on top of her head. "I'm Nora O'Sullivan, and you must be the last of our guests, Lizzie and Mercy McCarthy."

"Hi, I'm Lizzie, and this is my sister Mercy."

"Your neighbor, Lolly, is right. You do look like twins, but you're different enough to tell you apart."

I grinned. Lolly, and her trusty dog Bernard, practically ran Shamrock Cove. And evidently she had already been gossiping about us. We didn't mind. She was a lovely woman and the queen of the court where we lived. There were six cottages on the court, and we'd come to adore our wonderful neighbors who lived there.

"Your castle is beautiful," Lizzie said.

The entry was massive, with a round table in the middle holding a huge vase full of colorful flowers. There was a humungous crystal chandelier overhead, and I wondered who had to dust it. Off to the right were two sets of armor. And the intricately carved banister was off to the right, too. The walls were painted a deep green and had wood detailing all around.

"Thank you. You've made it just in time for lunch. Let's get you settled," Nora said.

"Wait until you see the rooms," Rob whispered. "Straight out of an enchanted fairy tale."

"I love the gargoyles outside," Lizzie said.

"Those were added by one of our ancestors, who came from France. When she married into the family, she changed the inside and outside of the estate. We have her to thank for many of the adornments.

"Lolly said you two own the bookstore in Shamrock Cove now," she went on. "And I know that you, Mercy, are a fabulous writer. We've read all your books."

Even though I'd been a writer for most of my life, it was still difficult to accept praise. "Thank you, and we do."

"I knew your grandfather, Driscoll, he was a lovely man. He always seemed to know what book was right for me. I thought of him as kind of magical."

"Mercy has the same talent," Lizzie said.

"So do you," I added.

"Well, it seems you inherited it from him. I'm sorry I haven't been by yet. We've been so busy with opening the estate to visitors that I just fall into bed each night. But I will come visit soon to stock up. Besides, it might be nice to provide each room with more current reading. Many of our books are in French or Gaelic, and, while beautiful, they aren't exactly the thing for bedtime reading."

"We would love to have you," Lizzie said.

We followed Nora up the stairs and then down two long hallways, with Rob just behind as he had insisted on carrying our bags. We would need a GPS to navigate around the place. The woodwork on the walls was exquisite. It was difficult to find that sort of detail in more modern homes and estates. At the end of the row, she put an old-fashioned brass key into a door and twisted it open.

The room was huge with two four-poster beds. The canopies over them were made of a heavy blue brocade, which matched the curtains, chairs, and sofa. There was a fireplace flanked by large floor-to-ceiling windows.

"We call this the blue room," Nora said. "The loo is through there." She pointed to a door on the other side of the room. "Let us know if you need anything. I'll leave you to freshen up, as I need to check on lunch." She glanced at her watch. "Which will be in fifteen minutes in the main dining room. Here's a map of the castle." She pulled two pieces of paper from her pocket and handed us one each. "Feel free to explore, though we don't recommend going up to the third floor. We haven't renovated that yet. It's drafty and dusty up there."

"Thank you," I said. I was looking forward to the exploring part of the trip.

After she left, Rob sat on the edge of the bed. "So, what do you think?"

"It's not what I thought it would be," Lizzie said. "It's much bigger and more luxe."

"Wait until you see the rest," he said. "It will be perfect for the fancier fund-raisers our town throws. I'll leave you to it."

"Where is the dining room?" I asked.

"We've already checked the place out, but don't worry if you get lost. Just look for the central stairway. The dining room is to the right of the front door."

"Is our little gang the only guests here? I'm just curious how many rooms they have," I said.

Our little gang was Rob and his partner Scott, who lived next door. Brenna, who was a photographer, and lived on the other side of us. And Lolly, who lived in number six on our little court. And the local detective, Kieran, who had just moved into number five, but he had been too busy to come to Inishmore Castle with us.

"From what I counted on the map, there are nineteen suites. And besides our crew, there is a priest, a nun, and someone who calls herself a birder."

"A priest and a nun?" I asked. "It sounds like the beginning of a bad joke."

He laughed. "I guess they like their whiskey as well. We met them when we were coming in earlier. He's a bit stand-offish, and she was quiet. Rob and I suspect they didn't like us much."

"Then they are silly because you two are some of the best

humans we've ever met," I said. I couldn't stand any sort of prejudice. Rob and Scott were the most adorable couple and had become some of our best friends in Ireland. They were give-the-shirt-off-their-backs kind of people. We loved them.

He leaned in and kissed my cheek. "One of the many reasons we adore you both. I'll see you down there."

After we freshened up, it took a couple of minutes and two wrong turns to find the dining room.

Okay, Mr. Poe helped. All I had to say was, "Find the food." He led us straight to the dining room.

Our neighbors were lined up at a buffet and waved us in. After some quick hugs, we grabbed our food, which consisted of boxty, which was part potato and part bread, and coddle, which was like a sausage stew with even more potatoes. The latter wasn't the best-looking dish, but it had a wonderful taste.

We all sat down at the huge gothic-styled dining table. There were dragon heads on the chairbacks, and the table was ornately carved as well. Artwork that had to be several hundred years old covered the walls. There was a mix of portraits and sea vessels, along with landscapes.

I didn't miss that the priest and the nun sat as far away from us as possible and seemed to be having a tense conversation if their faces were any indication.

His black hair appeared as if he dyed it, and he had beady dark-brown eyes. There was something about him that seemed off.

And I'd never seen a nun who wore makeup.

"How's the writing going?" Brenna asked.

I rolled my eyes.

She laughed. "That good?"

"It is slow, which is why I decided to come along when Lizzie asked. A four-day weekend away from my computer sounded like a good idea. How was your shoot in Portugal?" She normally did business trade photography, but every once in a while, she'd book a job at some exotic locale. She was extremely talented.

"Magical. I know I'm thirty or more years from retirement, but I think it might be on my list. It was beautiful and the people were lovely."

"That's one of our places to visit," Lizzie said. "We've decided that once every few months we'll take a week, or at least a long weekend, to travel to places on our bucket list."

"By we, Lizzie means she, but I think it's a great idea," I said.

My sister bumped my shoulder. "You didn't fight me very hard on it."

Everyone smiled.

"Yes, because traveling to destinations we've dreamed about is such a drag."

"Why don't you introduce yourselves?" Lolly said to the other guests who sat near us.

There was a woman who looked to be in her twenties and was dressed from head to toe in khaki. "I'm Fiona," she said. "I'm a birder. I'm here for the wildlife and the whiskey." She winked and then laughed.

We joined her.

"We're Sally and Alex Airendale," a woman said. Her hair was in a perfect chignon and she wore diamonds around her neck and in her ears. "As you might notice from the accents, we're from America."

"How did you end up here?" Lolly asked. She was never shy with the questions and usually asked what we all wanted to.

"Business, for my husband," she said.

He nodded beside her.

"But I came along because who doesn't want to visit a castle?"

"And you?" Lolly said to a gentleman on the other side of the table.

"Maximillian Herbert, the O'Sullivans' accountant," he said.

"Oh?" Lolly seemed surprised.

"I thought it best I see how they are spending the allocated funds for the opening, so I can advise them." He seemed a bit self-important and spoke with a posh English, rather than Irish, accent.

Nora joined us and sat down at the head of the table. "I hope our estate is living up to your expectations," she said.

"Far surpassing it, to be honest," I said. "We've visited a few castles in Ireland and most of them are derelict or much smaller than one might imagine."

Our home in Shamrock Cove was in the bailey of a castle that sat up on the hill. That castle had been refurbished, but was a third of the size of Inishmore, and not nearly as grand on the inside.

A fork clattered onto a plate, and we all glanced down at the other end of the table. The priest was wagging a finger in the face of the nun, which didn't seem very priest-like. Her face was twisted in anger.

I wondered what that was about.

Lolly cleared her throat. "Nora, you should tell these youngsters some of the stories associated with the castle. Like the one about the buried treasure."

Nora smiled, seemingly grateful to Lolly for pulling the focus away from the pair at the other end of the table.

"As you might imagine, we have many stories about treasure and marauders who have been on the hunt for it. The rumors began in the late seventeen hundreds." She went on to tell us a couple of fascinating stories about the lords who lived in the castle and some of their not-so-happy arranged marriages.

"According to legend, there is a treasure stashed somewhere

in the castle. One of the former lords hid it from his wife and her family, thinking he would be safer from their murdering ways if they couldn't find it. He was wrong."

We all smiled.

While she spoke, I chanced a glance down to the priest and nun. They had stopped arguing to listen.

"We have a full weekend for you of whiskey tasting, cooking classes, art history lessons, gardening and so much more," Nora said. "You are, of course, welcome to attend everything, or whatever seems most interesting to you."

After lunch, we followed Nora out the back of the castle, through a rose garden, and down the hill to a large stone building shaped like a barn. The rain had paused, but she gave us umbrellas just in case. We'd also donned wellies in various colors to combat the muddy ground.

In Ireland, the constant rain was one of the reasons the place was so lush. We had the most beautiful garden around our home to prove it. Though, it was my sister who took care of most of it. I had a black thumb, and she was afraid for me to touch anything, lest I kill it.

Inside, the place was pristine. There were four huge copper stills wrapped in pipes and machinery. There were steps leading to walkways near the top of the stills.

"The distillery has been in the family since the seventeen hundreds," Nora said, "and has been in continuous production since then. Initially, the whiskey was only for the family. In the late nineteenth century, my husband's great-grandfather began distributing it locally, and we now sell it in the UK too.

"We're hoping to take the brand worldwide over the next five years as a way to help us preserve the estate and castle. As you might imagine, the upkeep here at Inishmore is quite expensive. We hope to open to tourists a few times a year and increase the distribution to help cover those costs. This is our first soft-open weekend. So, please let us know if there is anything we can do to make your stay better."

A man with gray hair, a white beard, and a handlebar mustache approached us.

"This is my husband, Gordon, the lead distiller, to take you through the tasting and tell you more about our Inishmore whiskey."

He smiled and shook our hands. When he went over to the priest and stuck out his hand, the priest didn't do the same. Gordon stared at him with a surprised look on his face.

Weird.

The nun kept her arms crossed but nodded at him. Her large black glasses covered most of her face.

Maybe they were afraid of germs.

"Follow me, and I'll show you where the fermenting process begins. We use malted and unmalted barley," he said. He pointed to machines that looked like giant bowls with lids. "Yeast converts to sugars and then become a liquid we call wash. This is when the alcohol is produced…"

An hour and a half later, I had the beginnings of a new book in mind. One that included a whiskey distillery and an angry priest. Throughout the tasting, Gordon and the priest kept glaring at each other as if they knew one another and it wasn't a pleasant reunion. Or perhaps because the priest seemed to be tasting more than his fair share of whiskey.

"I had no idea how difficult it was to make whiskey," Lizzie said on our way back to the castle. The rain had returned, and I could barely hear her over the thunder. "Also, I have a buzz."

"Me too," I said. Unlike wine tastings, where you sometimes spit it out after swishing it around in your mouth, part of the process with whiskey was the smoothness as it trickled down one's throat.

"It's grand I've got two handsome men to hold onto after those delicious wee drams," Lolly said, red-faced and grinning from ear to ear as Rob and Scott helped her up the path.

"If you lot would stop your incessant talking and move it along, we could make it back without us all getting drenched," the priest said as he bustled past us, rather unsteadily. The nun said nothing but was right at his heels.

"He might be a priest, but that man is just rude," Brenna said.

"I wonder why he's so grumpy," Lizzie said.

I shrugged. "No idea, but I feel sorry for his parishioners if that's how he acts with everyone. Can you imagine what it must be like for them to go to confession? What's that? You said a bad word? That will be five thousand Hail Marys."

She giggled, and I couldn't help but smile. Mr. Poe barked. He usually liked my jokes, which was just one more reason to love him.

Inside the mudroom off the kitchen, there were several benches where we could switch back to our shoes from our wellies.

"Did you enjoy the tour?" asked Nora, who was waiting for us.

"We did," Lizzie said, and the others all agreed.

"I found it fascinating," I said. "It's given me an idea for a book."

Nora clapped her hands. "Feel free to mention us. We could do with the publicity."

I didn't think my publisher would allow it, given I murdered people in my books, and they didn't like being sued. But I might be able to mention the brand if someone just drank it. Quite honestly, it was the best whiskey I'd ever tasted. I'd had my fair share through the years.

"I'll see what I can do."

. . .

Later that evening, we headed downstairs for cocktails—not that I planned to drink anything other than water. I still had a buzz from earlier in the afternoon. My sister and I had napped for an hour, and I still felt a bit bleary-eyed. If she hadn't insisted on my going downstairs with her, I would have happily slept until the next morning.

In my defense, I had had several sleepless nights stressing over deadlines because I was at a point in my book where I worried if I was doing it right. Every time I wrote a book, and there were many, this happened. The writer insecurity was never far away.

But now, I had a germ of an idea and I had the perfect way to work it into my current story. Lizzie had been right. All I needed was a break and a bit of inspiration from the whiskey distillery.

We met Scott and Rob downstairs in the foyer.

"Do you know which room the cocktails are in?" Lizzie asked them.

"The billiard room," Scott said. "But it isn't on the map we were given. We heard you coming and hoped perhaps you knew."

Mr. Poe yipped at our heels. Then he sniffed the air. He'd spent the afternoon warmly snug on Lizzie's bed, though she'd taken him for a walk an hour or so ago, while I had been getting ready.

He took off toward a hallway.

"Maybe he hears people," Lizzie said.

I often swore he was more human than dog, as he seemed to understand everything we said. He was smart and cute, which were two of the many reasons we adored him.

"We might as well follow him," I said. "He almost always knows where he's going before we do."

Halfway down the long hallway, he pawed at a pair of wooden doors. I opened one of them, expecting to find the billiard room and the rest of the guests. But when I did, it was a study. There were no lamps lit, but there was a figure sitting at the desk.

"Sorry to bother you, but can you tell us where the billiard room is?"

No answer.

Maybe he or she had headphones on. It was difficult to see, but there was definitely an outline silhouetted as lightning flashed outside the window.

"I'm sorry. We thought this was the billiard room," I said by way of apologizing. "So, uh. Right. I guess we'll leave you to your work. Sorry again for the interruption."

The figure didn't say anything.

Obviously, they didn't want to be bothered.

I shut the door, but Mr. Poe pawed it again and gave a sharp bark.

"What's wrong?" Lizzie asked. "That's his something is wrong bark."

"We both know that could mean a squirrel invading the garden," I said. It was true. The small furry dude took protecting his kingdom seriously.

"Come on, Mr. Poe. We need to find the others."

But he wouldn't budge. He just sat at the door and whined, then barked.

My sister and I stared at one another. She shook her head. "It can't be," she whispered. "Did you see anyone?"

I had. And the last time Mr. Poe had acted like this there had been a dead body on the other side of the door.

A chill slithered down my spine. Had the person on the other side of the door been hurt, or worse?

Not again. I had a habit of finding myself in a world of trouble without really trying.

"What's going on, and why are we whispering?" Scott asked.

"We think something bad might have happened," Lizzie said.

Their eyes went big. "I can go in first," Rob said.

"It's okay," I said. "It's probably nothing." In my head, I prayed it was mice that Mr. Poe had heard. Unfortunately, my Spidey senses said otherwise. Our brilliant dog wouldn't have bothered if he didn't think something was wrong.

I took a deep breath and opened the door again. I searched for a light switch but couldn't find one, so I pulled my phone out of my pocket and used the flashlight app.

After a few steps in, I stopped. I blinked, not believing what was before me.

"What is it?" Lizzie whispered. She was hanging back at the door.

Rob and Scott gasped as they saw what I had.

"It's the priest," I said. "And he's very dead."

TWO

While I was certain the priest was dead, I still checked his pulse. He didn't have one, and his body was cool to the touch. There was a pool of blood on the desk, most likely from the letter opener sticking out of his heart. His eyes were wide, as if he'd been surprised.

"What are you doing?" Lizzie asked from the doorway.

Rob and Scott had followed me in and stared down at the body in shock.

"Is there anything we can do?" Rob asked.

"We shouldn't touch anything," I said. "I'm certain he didn't stab himself, so the police will need to do forensics. Don't come any further into the room. We don't want to contaminate the scene."

That said, I fumbled around quickly to see if his cassock had pockets. It did. I pulled a tissue from my sweater and used it to slide out his wallet. Since Mr. Poe and I kept finding dead bodies, I really needed to start keeping a pair of crime scene gloves in my pocket.

"Why do you get to touch things?" Scott asked.

"And ew, you're touching a dead guy," Rob said.

"I'm being careful," I said. I flipped open the wallet. "Something about him bugged me from the get-go. I know priests are human and can be stern and unfriendly, but he seemed to go out of his way to be that way. I don't know what his wallet might tell us, but it's a start."

I should have immediately called the detective inspector, Kieran, who just happened to be Lolly's grandson. But once he arrived, I would no longer have access to the crime scene. I wish I had more control of my curiosity, but alas, I do not.

That curiosity gets me into trouble all the time.

There was a license with his picture. I took a photo with my phone so I could look him up later.

"Wait," I said. "When we were on the whiskey tour didn't Nora's husband call him Father Brennen?"

"I think so," Rob said.

"I wonder why his license says Carl Doyle. That's weird, right? Why would he change his name?"

"I think nuns do that when they marry God," Rob said. "But I'm not sure about priests."

"The bigger question is, why would someone kill him here? And the even bigger question is, why haven't you called Kieran?" my sister asked. "And has anyone thought about the fact there is a murderer in the castle?"

As she finished her sentence, there was a big boom of thunder, and we all jumped.

"You're right. We need to call Kieran," I said, as I stuffed the wallet back in the robes. I used my flashlight to scan the room once again. There were several books on the desk, as if he'd been doing some kind of research and I wondered what that was about. Nothing was turned over. There was no sign of a struggle. It was as if someone had stabbed him in the chest, and then he sat down at the desk.

I checked the carpet with my flashlight, and there was blood spatter on the floor near the curtains behind the desk.

There weren't any footprints, but the killer wouldn't have been able to avoid the blood spatter. It would be on their clothes.

"I don't get it," I said.

"What?" Rob asked.

The dead man's hands were palms up and surprisingly clean. "I could see him not struggling if someone had stabbed him from behind. But he had to see it coming. So why didn't he fight back? There should be defensive marks on his hands if he tried to stop the killer."

"That's something Kieran will need to figure out," Lizzie said. "You need to call him. Now."

It was time to bring the detective into the situation. Still, he would not be happy that we'd found another dead body. It had become common since we moved to the normally crime-free Shamrock Cove. We had a habit of showing up at the worst time.

Thunder rolled and there was a flash of lightning, and we all jumped again.

"This weather is wearing on my nerves," Rob said.

"Same," Lizzie said. "I'll find Nora and her husband to tell them what is happening. Promise me you'll let Kieran deal with this."

I nodded.

"Rob, you stay here with Mercy and the body. I'll go with Lizzie," the always sensible Scott said. "Until we know what's going on, I think we should travel in pairs."

"That's a good idea," I said.

I dialed Kieran on my cell, but there was no ring, only odd clicking sounds like something couldn't connect. "Darn," I said.

"What's wrong?"

"I don't have any bars. How about you?"

He glanced down at his cell and shook his head.

"There's a phone on the desk. Maybe they have a landline."

Using my tissue so that I didn't mess up any prints, I gingerly picked up the receiver. There was no dial tone.

"Anything?" he asked.

I shook my head.

"What do we do?"

"I have no idea. If all the lines are out, and the internet is down, we'll have no way of reaching him."

Outside the door I heard people talking excitedly. Nora and her husband entered. She put on the overhead lights and gasped.

"It's true," she said. "What do we do?" Tears streamed down her cheeks. "I don't understand."

"I tried to call the detective in Shamrock Cove, but the cell towers must be down," I said. "We tried the landline on the desk, but it didn't work either."

"That happens when we have storms," Gordon, her husband, said. "I'll drive into town and collect the detective."

"You can't go in this weather," his wife said. "It's too dangerous."

"I know, love, but he's dead. We can't just leave him like that until the storm clears," he said. "There is no telling how long that might be."

"I can come with you," Scott said.

Gordon nodded, and they took off.

"What should we do?" Nora asked.

"Go back to your guests and don't tell anyone what's happened. I'm going to stay here until the detective arrives," I said. "We need to make certain no one disturbs the scene."

Nora looked from the priest to me and shook her head. "I don't suppose there is any chance he just fell on that letter opener."

I understood her train of thought. She didn't want to think about a killer being in our midst.

"One can only hope," I said. "But I doubt it."

"I cannot believe this is happening. It's my worst nightmare come to life."

"It's not your fault," Lizzie said, and she put her hands on the other woman's shoulders. "My sister will figure this out. She's not just a great mystery writer, the police often have her consult on cases. She's helped solve quite a few murders."

Only by sheer dumb luck, but I had a feeling Lizzie would keep that bit to herself.

"Rob and I will stay here and make sure no one enters the crime scene while we wait for the detective."

"Are you sure?"

"Like Lizzie said, Mercy writes mystery books and works with the police on cases," Rob said. "She knows what to do and is quite knowledgeable about police procedures."

Nora glanced at each of us and nodded. "Thank you," she said. "I'm not sure how I can act like I haven't had the shock of a lifetime. I don't think I'm that good of an actress."

"Just think of playing your role as hostess. For everyone's sake, try to keep the guests together," I said. "Until we know what happened—well, it may not be safe. It is important to stay calm. You're doing it for your guests. It helps no one if people become hysterical."

I felt sorry for her. It was obvious she and her husband had gone to great lengths to refurbish the castle and the grounds. A bad review involving a murder on their first weekend wouldn't exactly be great for business.

"It is crazy this is happening. That poor man. He wasn't the nicest person, but no one deserves to go like that. And to think we have a killer here." She shivered, as did my sister.

Mr. Poe pawed at Lizzie's leg, and she scooped him up. He snuggled into her as if he sensed her unease. I don't think she even noticed what he was doing.

"What if someone asks where he is?" Nora said.

"Just say he's indisposed."

"That's a good idea," Rob said.

"Did you know much about him?" I asked. "Like, how did he come to be here? And did he and the nun, Sister Sarah, come together?"

"He booked his stay about a month ago," she said. "From what I understood, he was touring Ireland on holiday. And no, they didn't come together. She showed up the day after him. But..."

"But what?" I asked.

"Well, they did seem to know one another. They bickered like an old married couple, though I couldn't tell you what about. Anytime I came near them, they stopped talking. Do you think the nun killed him? Will I be struck down for blasphemy for even thinking that?"

"No," Lizzie and I said at the same time.

"You're only thinking what we all are," Lizzie said. "But it is all speculation, and it won't help the cause for us to think everyone is a suspect. Like my sister said, we have to act as if nothing has happened."

Well, that was interesting, though. Sister Sarah must have known the deceased. Perhaps she had a reason for killing him. Though, Kieran would insist we find proof before accusing anyone of anything. And right now, there was nothing I could see that would indicate who had killed him.

I knew many of the other guests. They were our friends and neighbors. The Airendales and the birder, Fiona, hadn't seemed to take much notice of the arguing priest and nun. Neither had Maximillian Herbert, the O'Sullivans' accountant.

Had Sister Sarah killed him? It would have taken a great deal of force to push that blade into the heart. But what would have been her motive? It was too easy to blame someone, and investigators needed evidence, not supposition. If she did kill him, though, blood would be all over her clothing. That would be easy enough to prove.

Nora sniffed. "I'm not certain I can do this."

Lizzie cleared her throat. "I'll be there to help you. We only have to get through drinks and dinner. We'll pretend nothing has happened. That'll be safest for all of us. If a killer thinks we're suspicious, that's when bad things happen. In these instances, I've discovered it is best to play dumb."

The other woman nodded and let Lizzie guide her away.

"Who do you think killed him?" Rob whispered as the lights flickered out.

"Well, it wasn't one of us—at least, I hope not. From the sound of things, he and the nun didn't get along and they knew each other. But if she's a real nun—"

"What?"

"Well, they are married to God, and I just can't see someone of her stature being able to drive that letter opener through the ribs and up into the heart. The angle would be nearly impossible, even for a fully grown, much larger man."

He grunted. "So, maybe the nun didn't do it."

"It's suspicious that his name doesn't match the one he gave the O'Sullivans. Was he hiding? And why? And why was he in this study?" Trying to stay away from the crime scene as much as possible, I perused the room with only the light from my phone. There were many books on the shelves, but everything appeared in order. Though I couldn't see the ones at the top where the shelves met the ceiling.

"He was British according to his license. What was he doing here in Ireland in the middle of nowhere?"

I had so many questions.

"It sounds like one of your mystery novels with priests and nuns as the bad guys."

The lights suddenly flashed back on. I was near the body and took some pictures. Gruesome, yes. But I had no idea when Kieran would show up so this was my only chance to take a good look.

That's when I noticed the rosary in his hand.

It looked like the same one that Sister Sarah wore around her neck. It was broken, as if he'd ripped it off her.

I smiled. "I don't normally use any sort of religious archetypes for fear of alienating readers, but something tells me these two are not who they pretend to be."

"Really?" His eyes went wide.

I nodded. "It's the name. I think he was pretending. I mean, if you're going on the run, no one pays attention to you if you're clergy, right? People just assume you are a decent guy when they see you in the robes and collar. I wish the internet wasn't down so I could search his name."

"You think all that because the names don't match?"

I shrugged. "It's all supposition. You've met me. I look at situations through a writer's brain first. And he didn't seem to be a decent guy. Not that someone from the church has to be. It's just that he appeared to be very guarded and kind of nasty. He argued with the nun, so there was something not right there. And look at that." I pointed to the rosary.

"Is that hers?"

"I saw her wearing it, but we won't know until we ask her."

"You can't ask her questions. Kieran will kill you."

I laughed. "You've met me. I can't always contain my curiosity."

"And you think the nun is also pretending?"

I pursed my lips. "I have no idea. But one thing has bothered me since we first met her."

"What's that?" he asked.

"How many nuns do you know who wear lipstick?" I'd noticed the pink lipstick earlier when I'd first seen her at lunch. I was fairly certain nuns had to give up all worldly goods, and makeup would be part of that. Though, since she'd said to the owners she was on vacation, maybe she'd treated herself. "That and the rosary in his hand make me suspicious of her.

"Still, I can't see her having the strength to kill him like this. She would have to be unnaturally strong."

"See, that's why you are good at this sort of thing. I hadn't even noticed her face. I think I saw the habit and figured she'd look down on Scott and me, and I didn't want to give her the chance to say something nasty—or give us one of those condescending looks."

"Well, that's her loss. To know you is to love you. And if they were good people, they should be accepting of everyone, especially you and Scott."

"Thanks, friend."

"I'm going to take a quick look around. If you see anyone coming, whistle or something."

He laughed. "Kieran will be mad if you mess anything up."

"I won't touch anything. But I can't just stand here doing nothing."

"Okay. I'll be your lookout." He crossed over towards the doorway.

I moved slowly around the study, searching for any more clues. The furniture was upright, and nothing much seemed out of place. Well, except for the dead guy. The spatter of blood near the curtains continued to spread on the rug.

It made me wonder if someone had been hiding behind the curtains and had surprised him. Perhaps he'd even been sitting, and they stabbed him. I stared at the letter opener in his chest. The angle was wrong. The letter opener must have been razor-sharp and strong enough to go through the breastbone. And the angle was slightly upward as if someone knew what they were doing.

Stabbing someone in the heart wasn't as easy as it appeared.

He must have died instantly, or there would be much more blood. So, the perpetrator stabbed him, and maybe the priest stumbled into the chair. Forensics would have a better idea.

But since the angle was upward, the killer could have been

shorter. Or, maybe, they just knew what they were doing. The same thoughts kept rolling around in my head.

Neither scenario helped my nerves. The thunder boomed even louder, and the lights flickered out again.

"Someone's coming," Rob whispered.

I quickly moved into the doorway as if I'd been there the whole time. A very wet Scott and Gordon came down the hallway.

"Where's Kieran?"

Scott shook his head. "The bridge connecting to the main road back to town is underwater. We couldn't get across."

"So, he isn't coming?" Rob asked.

"No one will be able to get through until the storm stops," Gordon said. "It's a nightmare out there. We are used to the flooding, but it is a fair nuisance when it's this bad."

"It's raining so hard you can't see three feet in front of the car," Scott said. "If Gordon didn't have quick reflexes, we would have landed in the river."

Rob went pale, and he gently grabbed Scott's arm.

"I'm okay," Scott said, patting his partner's hand.

"But what do we do now?" Gordon asked. His face was red, and his voice harsh, as if he were angry. What I couldn't tell was whether it was because this might have ruined their opening weekend, or whether he hated the priest. "Do we just leave him until the police can get here? Shouldn't we move the body to a freezer or something? Out of all the things I thought might go wrong this weekend, this was not one of them."

"Well, I've worked with the police, and I've done a lot of research as a writer. For right now, we need to leave the body where it is. It is cool enough in the castle to keep it from decomposing too quickly," I said. "We shouldn't move anything in a crime scene. We want everything to appear exactly as we found it.

"We'll need to stand guard until Kieran and his team can

get here. We can't risk the killer coming back and removing evidence. Do we have any idea when the storm will end?"

"Not until early morning and who knows when the bridge will be passable," Gordon said. "We'll need to wait for the water to go down. I can take first watch."

"Uh. Actually, why don't you let me do that," I said.

"But you're a woman. It isn't right."

Scott and Rob's eyes went wide.

I cleared my throat. "I am. I also understand how to preserve a crime scene. Kieran trusts me, and I think he'd prefer if I stayed."

Or he'd be furious that I'd inserted myself into the situation. One never knew when it came to the detective inspector. Kieran could be a bit overprotective at times, but I'd realized a few months ago that it was only because he cared.

Poor Gordon didn't need to know all of that. He had enough to stress about.

"Like we've said before, she has worked with the detective inspector on several cases," Rob said. "And even solved a few."

Gordon appeared confused. "But I thought you were a writer. It's my home and my responsibility."

"Let us help," I said. "Kieran will appreciate that you've done your best. And like I said, he trusts me. It's best to help your wife distract the rest of the guests. I mentioned that they should say the priest is indisposed for now. We'll set up right here in the doorway with the door shut, so the killer will have no idea we are in here."

And hopefully, the murderer wouldn't be coming back.

"We'll sit with her," Scott said. "She won't be alone. You can tell the others we had a bit too much of your fine whiskey."

I hid my smile. They were quite protective of Lizzie and me.

"If you're sure," Gordon said. The poor man seemed like he didn't want to leave. Did that make him guilty? I couldn't tell.

"We are," I said. "You can help us by keeping the other guests away from this area."

He rubbed his hand through his hair and frowned. "We haven't had a murder here since the early eighteen hundreds. I can't believe this has happened."

"Did you know the priest?" I asked.

He shook his head. "Only as a guest. He had a lot of questions about the property and was very interested in the castle's history. He wanted to see all the books, and we'd let him use the study since many of the volumes are in here, as well as in the main library. I just thought he was a history buff."

Well, that explained why he'd been in the room.

"Was there anything strange about him?" I asked.

"What do you mean?"

I'd stuck my foot in my mouth. "Did he give you any reason to think he might be up to something shady?"

Gordon frowned. "He was a priest," he said, as if that explained everything.

"Right. Well, you should probably check on Nora and the guests. We'll stand guard."

The lights flickered out again throwing us into darkness, and there was a scream.

Great. Now what?

THREE

I turned on the flashlight on my phone, and my friends did the same. "Could you tell where the scream came from?" I asked.

They shook their heads.

"Gordon, you and I will go investigate," I said. "Rob, do you and Scott mind staying here until I can get back?" I really didn't want to risk leaving the body unattended in case the killer returned. For all I knew, this could be a diversion to get us away from the scene of the crime.

"Is she always this bossy?" Gordon asked.

"Yes," Scott and Rob replied at the same time. "But it comes in handy. We'll cover things here. You go investigate the scream."

Gordon and I headed down the long hallway.

"Besides our crew, how many others are here for the weekend?" I asked. We passed several rooms and doors that were closed. This place never seemed to end. If it weren't for Gordon, we would have been lost long ago.

"That's my wife's side of things, but I think we have thirteen, including your group. Well, I guess twelve now. I cannot believe this has happened. It's such a shock, and it hasn't sunk in yet. My poor wife." He sighed. "She's worked so hard to turn the family enterprises around. If it weren't for her, we would have lost all of this years ago."

The ornate sconces along the hallway flickered off and on, and Gordon kept his flashlight on as he guided us along the way.

"But it's your family's legacy."

He nodded. "Since the day we married, she's taken it all on her shoulders. I'm a distiller at heart. Everything else is all her. She came up with the business ideas and revamped the estate. It has taken years, and this was supposed to be the weekend of her dreams. My heart is broken for her. I love her and I wish she didn't have to deal with all of this."

He was sweet and sincere. He dearly loved his wife. And though I hadn't taken him off my suspect list, I couldn't imagine him doing something that might upset Nora.

"And how long has the castle been open as a hotel?"

"Only a month or so. We did some trial runs to make certain we had the right number of staff and could handle the business. This is the first official weekend for all our events and classes.

"We've been doing the whiskey tastings for years, though. But visitors would only come for the tastings and then leave."

"And do you know any of the guests this weekend personally?"

"No. Well, apart from our accountant, Maximillian, and Lolly. She and my ma were friends for years. Bless her soul." He made the sign of the cross. "I've known Lolly my whole life, and she and my wife have become friends. It was Lolly's suggestion to invite your group to help spread the word. And now, all of this has happened. We'll never get off the ground."

"I don't think you need to worry about that. We're good and fair people. This place is gorgeous. And this death isn't your fault." At least, I hoped not. "And you didn't know the priest?" I went on.

"No. He was a guest just like the others. Like I said, he asked a lot of questions. But mostly he's been keeping himself to himself. He asked for access to the books in the study. We didn't see any reason to say no."

"That's odd, right? Why was he so interested in those old books? I mean, if he was a priest."

"You think he was misrepresenting himself?" Gordon's eyes opened wider in surprise.

Once again, I'd stuck my foot in my mouth by not curbing my thoughts. I had a tendency to talk to myself so much, that sometimes those words came out around others. It was my writer's brain trying to figure things out. I decided to switch the subject.

"How did you and your wife meet?"

"Oh, we were wee ones. Our mothers were friends and both great gardeners. My wife followed in her mother's footsteps and brought her love of nature to the estate when we wed."

I smiled. "How long have you been married?"

"We're going on thirty years. We were friends most of our lives but didn't start dating until she came home from university. She has quite a business mind. I'd been so focused on the distillery that I'd let the rest of the estate go. But she turned things around. Mind you, if she hadn't come up with this hospitality idea, we would have lost it all."

"She sounds brilliant." I loved that he was so proud of his wife and her business sense. The appreciation of her was evident in his voice. "But you have all this art on the walls, and antiquities. Could you not sell some of those?"

He shrugged. "It isn't worth as much as you might think."

I wondered what he meant by that.

"Anyway, you're right. She is brilliant. Part of me feels guilty for pulling her into all of this."

"Why is that?"

"There have always been rumors that this place was cursed, and there are times when I believe it. Like tonight."

"You can't blame yourself for what happened."

He shrugged. "It occurred under my watch. The fortunes of our family have been up and down throughout history. Just about every one of my relatives has died in an odd sort of way. My wife's family seems to have fallen under that curse."

"I thought the castle was built just a few hundred years ago." It was odd to say, just a few, when most buildings in Ireland were older than anything we had in America.

"Even though we have turrets, it is legally considered an estate. And it was built by French noblemen. But everyone has always called it a castle."

"You mentioned your wife's family. What happened to them?"

"That was some bad business. Her parents were killed in a boating accident off the coast of Spain while on holiday—has to be nearly twenty years or so ago."

"Oh, that's terrible."

The lights flickered back on, and I had to blink against the brightness.

"It was," he said. "The boat capsized, and the authorities never discovered how or why. Like I said, odd deaths. It crushed my poor Nora, but she's a strong one and so brave."

I admired his appreciation for his wife. While I hadn't spent much time with her, I'd taken an instant liking to her. She reminded me of Lizzie. Someone with an open heart who welcomed strangers.

We turned a corner at the end of the hall, and he made his way across the expansive entryway to a pair of double doors.

The lights flickered but stayed on as we entered the dining room. The place was filled with candles, and several guests stood around someone at the head of the table. They blocked the view so I couldn't see who it was.

"What happened?" Gordon asked worriedly. "We heard someone scream."

The guests parted, and we found Sister Sarah sitting in a chair, looking quite pale. Her foot was propped up on a small stool with a small bag of ice on her ankle.

"She says someone pushed her down the stairs," Nora whispered. Her face was pinched with worry. "Sister Sarah, I'm so sorry this happened to you. Tell me what you need."

I glanced over her shoulder to my sister, who had a perplexed look on her face.

"Ouch," Sister Sarah said as she tried to move her leg. She appeared to be in great pain. But all I could think about was how had her broken rosary ended up in a dead man's hand? Her habit was disheveled, and a peek of curly blonde hair showed through. It was obviously dyed an unnatural color.

I motioned for Lizzie to come away from the crowd.

"What's going on?" I asked. "Did you see what happened?"

"Mr. Poe and I were in the entryway trying to figure out which door led to the nearest bathroom," she whispered. She stopped and glanced back over her shoulder.

"And?"

"I was coming out of the first room off the entry, which was not the bathroom, when I heard the scream. The lights were out, and it was so dark. There was the scream, and then I saw something white on the floor. It was her habit. I used my light on my phone and saw her sprawled out on the floor."

"She says she was pushed," I said.

Lizzie pursed her lips. "That's the thing. I was right there. I didn't hear her fall, and I certainly didn't hear anyone else on the stairs. They're wooden. Anytime you go up or down, it sounds like a herd of cows. And everyone except for you all came rushing out of the dining room when they heard the scream. Who could have pushed her?"

"Are you saying she lied?" I whispered the question.

Her eyes went wide. "Of course not, she's a nun. Why would she lie?"

I shrugged. "She doesn't act like any nun I've ever met, not that there have been that many." But I'd done my fair share of charity work when I lived in the States. And nuns were usually at the forefront of creating schools and activities for the under-privileged near where I had lived in Manhattan. "Did you see her ankle?"

Lizzie shook her head. "She insisted on putting the ice on top of her stocking, so we couldn't see anything. If she was lying, why would she do that?"

"To distract us," I said. "And perhaps to draw any suspicion from herself regarding the priest. I mean, they did seem to know one another, and they were seen fighting more than once. But if she were doing that, why?"

She bit her lip. "Do you realize what you're saying?"

"That she is lying for some reason? Yes. But, like I said, the big question is why. It feels hinky no matter what."

"Is Kieran here?"

I shook my head. "The bridge is underwater, and we have no cell or internet service at the moment. The cavalry can't get here. The rain doesn't look like it will stop anytime soon."

She frowned and then blew out a breath. The breath was a sign she was trying to control her emotions. "Oh, dear. What are we going to do?"

I patted her arm. "Don't worry. We'll figure it out. And the storm should pass by morning. Gordon and I left Rob and Scott to keep an eye on the room with the body. I don't want to risk the killer coming back to change or hide anything. We can't be too careful, though. When we are in the larger groups, I need you to keep your eyes and ears open for anything suspicious."

She shivered. "Why does this sort of thing keep happening?"

I shrugged. "I have no idea. We do seem to find ourselves in the middle of trouble wherever we go. Just lucky, I guess." I tried to make a joke, but she didn't smile.

"Nora's been talking about their resident ghosts," Lizzie said. "She has so many stories that sound true I started to believe ghosts were real. My nerves were already on edge when we heard the scream."

I smiled. "I don't know about ghosts, but the family does have its fair share of unexplained deaths, according to Gordon, that is."

"Really?"

I nodded.

"I know I've probably asked this already, but do you have any idea why someone would have wanted to kill the priest?"

I shook my head. "No. Except for the fact I don't think he was a priest any more than Sister Sarah is a nun. That's one of the reasons I came with Gordon to check on the scream. I was hoping to speak to some of the other guests. Is anyone suspicious about the priest?"

"No. I don't think anyone has noticed he isn't here."

We moved back over to the others who were still circled around Sister Sarah, holding the bag of ice on her ankle. She winced a few times but was she really hurt? I wasn't so certain.

"Madam, are you ready for dinner?" a woman asked from the doorway.

Nora looked around the room as if she wasn't certain what to do. She appeared near tears, and I didn't blame her. It had been a crazy night and she was trying to pretend that there wasn't a dead guy in her study.

"I could do with some food," Lolly said, taking over. "I think we all could." She was good at that sort of thing. She was one of the kindest women I'd ever met, but she had an authoritative voice. And I'd never seen anyone argue with her.

"Right, then," Nora said. "Cook, we are ready."

The American couple and our neighbor Brenna helped to

position Sister Sarah's chair and the stool her foot rested on so she could face the table. I sat down on the right side of the nun with my sister next to me. Lolly and Brenna sat on the other side.

The soup course was one of my favorites, Colcannon with potatoes. The nun clasped her hands and bowed her head. She whispered some words. Lolly bowed her head as well, and we followed suit.

The words she said didn't sound like any prayer I'd ever heard. But who was I to judge? Still there was something odd about her. When she stopped her prayer, we raised our heads.

The soup was hearty and quite tasty. I hadn't realized I was so hungry. I felt a bit guilty for leaving Rob and Scott behind, but this was my chance to have some casual conversations with the other guests.

"I'm sorry to hear about your accident," I told the sister. "I hope your ankle will be okay."

"Wasn't an accident, I tell you. I was pushed. I'm lucky to be alive. I'll be covered in bruises tomorrow."

Bruises no one would be able to see since she was covered from head to toe.

That was terrible to think, but I believed my sister. If she thought the nun was faking the accident, then she was. Lizzie was always aware of her surroundings. Unlike me, who was often lost in thought as characters spoke in my head. I had to force myself to be in the present. And this was one of those times when I needed to be aware.

"But you didn't see anyone?"

"It was pitch-black," the nun said angrily. "How was I supposed to see anything? There was no light."

"Maybe it was a gust of air," Brenna offered. She was super-model beautiful and reminded us of Lupita Nyong'o. She was just as gorgeous on the inside and had become a lovely and dependable friend. "The castle does have odd drafts. I felt one on the second-floor staircase and in my room. It was so strong it lifted the bottom ruffle of my shirt. And the windows were closed tight."

She shivered.

"Maybe it was one of the ghosts they keep talking about," Fiona, the birder, said from Brenna's other side. "I've been reading the pamphlets, and they talk about all the restless spirits who live here. Centuries of them. Nora has been sharing some of those stories, as well." She sounded like she believed what she was saying.

Lizzie and I stared at one another.

"Most likely drafts," Lolly said in her practical way. "Mind you, we Irish are a superstitious lot, but this place is drafty as they come. It doesn't matter how many improvements they do. It's the way the place was originally built to carry air throughout during warmer months. Even with proper heating, there are going to be drafts."

Everyone tucked into their soup.

"Sister, how did you hear about the castle? Did you come with Father Brennen?" I asked, even though I knew the answer. I was curious about what she might say.

Her jaw tightened.

That wasn't suspicious at all.

"No. I've never met him before," she said offhandedly.

"Oh, I saw you, uh, chatting during the whiskey tour. I thought you knew one another."

"No," she said sternly. "I came on my own. My order is thinking about creating a business making soap. I came to see how they ran things here. Mind you, we wouldn't be having guests stay. But they could tour our facilities and shop."

"Oh, that sounds interesting," Lizzie said. "What kind of soap?"

The sister gave her a hard stare. I would have given millions to know what was going through the woman's head.

"Soap using goat's milk. There may also be a skincare line if we are successful in our initial efforts." She sounded rehearsed. Something wasn't right about her.

Or maybe my imagination was in overdrive.

That happened sometimes. My brain never stopped trying to write books. I could find inspiration for stories everywhere I looked.

But this was a real murder and I had to separate fiction from fact. The nun was at the top of my list. Even though I had none of that pesky evidence Kieran would insist was necessary.

He was right. I tended to go more by my gut. And it said Sister Sarah was up to no good.

The rain pounded against the stained-glass windows, and the wind howled around the castle, making an eerie sound. I shivered.

The servants cleared our plates. The next course was a delicious corned beef brisket with garlic cabbage and peas.

"Nora, where is Father Brennen?" the nun asked after a few minutes of uncomfortable silence as we ate. For someone who didn't know the man, she seemed extremely curious. And it seemed like she might be trying to draw attention away from herself.

Nora went a bit white and choked on her beef. "Uh, he's indisposed," she said quickly.

The nun stared down the table suspiciously, which raised the hackles on my spine. I'd always wondered about that phrase, but I understood it now.

"Where exactly is your order?" I asked. The words came out a bit sharply, and Lizzie nudged me with her elbow. "I mean, it's just that you don't sound Irish."

"I'm not. I'm British. Cornwall," she said, without turning to look at me.

"I hear it's lovely there," Lizzie said. "I've always wanted to visit the coast. Maybe we can take a vacation there next year and visit your nunnery if you have your business up and running by then."

My sister sounded sweet and positive. But I could tell she was trying to dig a little further.

The nun nodded but didn't bother saying anything.

Between the makeup and the dyed hair, I would bet a dozen doughnuts this woman was no nun, and that she had murdered the priest. Or at the very least she'd been involved. The rosary she'd been wearing earlier was in the dead man's hand.

Now, I just had to prove it.

FOUR

When the meal was over, I discreetly asked Nora if I could have food sent to Rob and Scott's room. Since I planned on taking the first watch overnight, I wanted them to get some rest.

Lizzie went back to the study with me and insisted on staying. Neither of us wanted to actually sit in the room with the dead body. It had nothing to do with the creepiness, and everything to do with the smell of death.

But we didn't have a choice. We sat on the floor next to the closed door.

"Why can't we sit on the chairs?" Lizzie asked.

"If the murderer sat down in one of them, they may have left some DNA. I don't want to disturb the crime scene more than we already have."

"Oh, that makes sense." We leaned back against the wall of bookcases. It had been a long day, and my sister nodded off about an hour into our vigil. Mr. Poe snored softly by her side.

The storm was still raging outside, but I kept trying to connect with Kieran, our local detective. It took almost three hours, but I finally heard a ringtone.

"Mercy? What's wrong?" Kieran asked sleepily. I mean, it was three in the morning, I couldn't blame him.

"We're at Inishmore Castle," I said.

"I know. Is Gran okay?" he asked worriedly. Lolly was his grandmother and she'd helped raise him when he was younger.

"Yes. Everyone from the court is okay. But one of the guests was murdered. A priest."

There was a long pause on the other end. "The phone cut out. Did I hear murder?"

"Yes." There was nothing but static. "The owner, Gordon, and Scott tried to come and get you, but the bridge is flooded. Only a few of us know what happened. And we've been guarding the door so the killer can't get back in to mess with the evidence."

"And you've put a target on your back. Why didn't you just lock it?"

"Because I don't know who we can trust, and someone might have a set of keys."

"Talk me through how you know it's a murder."

"He had a very fancy letter opener through his heart. I don't think he accidentally fell onto it."

"Right. How did you find him?"

"This place is enormous, and we were a bit lost. Mr. Poe scratched at the door. And, well, we found the body."

"I may need to hire your dog for the force."

I smiled. Mr. Poe adored Kieran. Whenever the detective inspector was around, Mr. Poe demanded attention from him. Kieran tried to act like our dog was a menace, but his smiling and giving him lots of pets spoke otherwise.

"Please tell me you haven't been asking questions of the other guests."

I sighed. "I don't want to lie to you."

He groaned. "Once again, putting a target on your back. How many times do we need to have this conversation?"

"You can yell at me later. Tell me what we should do."

"Nothing. I'll be there soon."

"How? It's still raining, and everything is flooded."

"I will be there as soon as I can. Be careful." His phone cut out, and there was nothing but static.

"What did he say?" Lizzie asked sleepily.

"Well, he wasn't happy we've found a dead body yet again. But basically, he said to hold tight and not to ask any more questions."

"That seems sensible."

I laughed. "You always agree with him."

"Well, if it keeps someone from trying to kill you, then yes I do."

"I haven't asked you, but do you remember seeing the priest talking with anyone other than Sister Sarah?"

She yawned and then picked up Mr. Poe, who snuggled into her.

"I was with you, so we saw the same things," she said. "I'll be honest, something about him was off-putting. And it wasn't just his attitude or that he yelled at us. You know how you get a sense of someone? I'm embarrassed to say, without knowing him at all, that I didn't like him. I was thinking that men like him gave priests a bad name."

"Don't feel guilty. I felt the same way."

"Do you think he was really a priest?"

"No. And I don't think Sister Sarah is a nun."

Her eyes went wide. "Why not?"

"She wasn't happy when I asked what order she was from and pointed out she wasn't Irish."

"She's a religious person," Lizzie said. "Maybe she just didn't like talking about herself."

"You may be right. But remember, she and the priest were arguing. She made a point of asking about him at dinner, and it felt like she was trying to draw attention away from herself. She didn't seem surprised either when it was mentioned he was indisposed. Her eyes narrowed, like she knew we weren't telling the truth. That and when she prayed at dinner, it didn't sound like she knew what she was saying. It was a bunch of random words.

"You were chatting with some of the other guests at dinner, did you notice anything suspicious?"

"No. The American couple, the Airendales, are celebrating their seventh anniversary. They both enjoy a bit of whiskey, at least, that is what the wife told me. She seemed kind of posh. And did you notice those diamonds she wears? They seem more appropriate for a gala than a weekend dinner on vacation. But I'm not judging. She mostly talked about shopping and the art here in the castle."

My sister didn't realize how her naturally affable way drew people to her. Other folks told her things without her prying much. She'd always been like that.

The lights flickered back on. I blinked against the brightness. They'd been going off and on all night. I felt better when they were on, even though the dead body was easier to see.

Two hours later, there was a loud noise on the other side of the door. We opened it to find several people coming down the hallway.

My eyes were bleary, but I could see that Kieran led the crowd. He was damp, they all were, but he was still ruggedly handsome. We'd spent a lot of time together the last few months discussing cases, and he'd become a fantastic resource for my books.

While he'd never admit it, I'd become a sounding board for him as well. We met at the pub in Shamrock Cove several nights a week to discuss cases. My sister called them dates. But she was much more romantically minded than I was.

He'd brought his sergeant, Sheila, and what looked like a forensic team.

Lizzie and I moved out of the study.

"You go on to bed. I'll be up soon," I said.

She glanced from me to Kieran. "Are you sure?"

I nodded. "No reason for both of us to lose more sleep."

"I think I'll wait for you," she said.

Rob and Scott were coming down the hallway from the other way. It was time for them to take over the watch.

"Can you two take Lizzie to our room?"

"No." My sister wasn't usually so stubborn. "I'm waiting for you."

Our friends looked from me to my sister and then at Kieran. Lizzie might be the quieter of the pair of us, but she wasn't a person to be messed with and she was making that clear for some reason.

"I can't believe you made it, Kieran," Rob said. "How did you know?"

The detective inspector nodded toward me. "Mercy called. It wasn't easy to get here. Now, tell me everything," he said to me.

I explained in detail what I hadn't been able to tell him on the phone. "Since we found him, someone has been guarding the room so the killer couldn't come back."

"I don't suppose you thought about what would happen if the killer did come back and found you here?"

I shivered. I tended to be single-minded and not really worried about myself when murder was involved. I had no idea what I would have done if the killer had returned, other than protecting my sister with my life.

It just hit me that I'd put us both in danger by staying with the body.

"No," I said. "Not really. I thought we were doing a good thing so that no one messed with any evidence."

He sighed. He knew me well enough that it wasn't worth arguing about me doing things that might have put mine and my sister's lives in danger. I didn't do it on purpose. I was just trying to do the right thing.

"When was the last time either of you saw him alive?"

"We were down at the distillery doing a tasting," I said.

"Don't forget about him fighting with the nun," Lizzie said. "They seemed to be having a rather emotional conversation. And Mercy thinks they aren't really clergy."

"Oh? And when was that? When you saw them fighting?" he asked.

"When we were coming back from the tasting," she said. "Neither of them seemed to be particularly nice. We tried to speak to Sister Sarah at dinner, but she wasn't happy about it. Mercy is right. There is something strange about her. Every time we asked a personal question, she changed the subject."

I couldn't stifle my smile.

Kieran shook his head. "That is interesting, but she may prefer not to talk about herself. It doesn't make her guilty of murder."

My sister shrugged. "Never said she did it. Only that Mercy thinks she's up to something hinky."

"Hinky?" Kieran asked as he looked at me.

"I know you like evidence, but my gut says something weird was going on between them."

"Right. And when you first walked in to the study, what did you see?"

I took him through the events. "According to Gordon, he'd been interested in the history of the estate. That's why he was in here. When we arrived, he was just sitting in the chair with the letter opener in his chest," I said. "Since it was probably on the desk, I'd say it was a crime of opportunity."

Kieran opened his mouth, but I held up a hand.

"I know. We need evidence. We didn't touch anything,

including the furniture in case you need to check for fibers or DNA, but I did search the bookshelves. Nothing seemed out of place."

"Right, Detective Mercy," he joked. "Go get some rest. This is going to take a while. And in future, please leave the interrogations to me."

"We will," Lizzie said as she hooked her arm in mine.

"How did you get across the river?" I asked.

"I walked on water," he grumbled.

Lizzie giggled.

"Emergency boats," Sheila said next to him.

That made more sense. Though it was unusual for Kieran to make any sort of joke, and I couldn't help but smile.

The team paused to put on coverup suits and gloves. Then they went into the study.

"This is going to take a few hours. Like I said, go get some rest. We can talk later," Kieran said.

"Come on, Mercy. I'm exhausted." My sister pulled me down the hallway. "Now we have to figure out how to get back to our room," she said.

Rob and Scott had already gone back up, so we were on our own. But I had been keeping track of our movements through the castle.

"Right. Left. Up the stairs and to the right again," I said.

"Thank goodness you were paying attention."

When we reached the second floor, Mr. Poe growled in Lizzie's arms.

"What is it?"

I turned to look behind us. I had a strange feeling that someone was watching us.

My sister followed my glance over her shoulder. "Is someone there?"

I didn't want to spook her. She'd been through enough the last few hours.

"Nothing. I was just curious about why Mr. Poe was growling."

"You know him, it could be squirrels outside. He seems to hear everything. Besides, this is an old place with lots of creaks."

"True," I said.

The lights flickered out again. I felt sorry for Kieran and his team trying to work the crime scene in the dark.

There was a weird groaning sound down the hallway.

My sister shivered in the light from my phone.

"Has to be the wind," I said.

"Right," she said. "Or one of those ghosts Nora keeps talking about." She was joking, but I could tell from her tone that she was nervous.

Who could blame her? It had been one strange night.

We hurried to our room and locked the door quickly behind us. Then we changed into our PJs.

We'd been lying in our beds for a few minutes, but I couldn't seem to calm down. Too much had happened.

"You're thinking too hard," Lizzie said.

"You know it's the way my brain works."

"Yes. But I also know if you get some rest, you'll be a lot more on it later today. You know how you are. Even if Kieran did ask you not to ask questions, you'll want to be fully aware and ready to roll."

"That sounds like a bad line from a cop show."

She laughed, but it wasn't a happy sound.

"Maybe we'll wake up to find Kieran has solved the case," I said, more for her benefit than mine. "He might get lucky and the killer left fingerprints on the letter opener."

"That's more positive than I've ever heard you be." She yawned.

I smiled.

"Do you believe in curses?" Lizzie asked. "When I spoke to Nora, she said the family has had a stream of bad luck over the last five hundred years or so. Even before the castle was built."

"No. I don't believe in curses. I think some people just do the pile-on theory," I said.

"What do you mean?"

"Well, like with us. After what happened to Mom, and then the accident not long after that." Lizzie's fiancé and his daughter had been killed in an auto accident six months after our mom died from cancer. Our moving to Ireland had been to get a fresh start.

And except for my new habit of finding dead bodies, we'd adjusted well here. We loved our home and neighbors, and Lizzie loved running our grandfather's bookstore.

We had a good life.

"Sorry I brought that up," I said.

"No. It's okay. We're supposed to talk about the past." Lizzie sniffed. "But you're saying we could say we were cursed because those things happened one after another. And then we discovered a grandfather we never knew who left us his home and store. But we didn't get to meet him because he died too. And we have a father, who may or may not be dead."

"Right. Someone might pile all those things together and think we'd had a bit of bad luck," I said. "But, in truth, life has ups and downs. Most people aren't aware of their family's five-hundred-year-old history like Gordon and Nora. So, they can pile on with those big life events. But the truth is, life really does have peaks and valleys.

"Take their financial woes, which are more indicative of the times we live in than any curse. Lots of businesses are having trouble, and Nora and Gordon admitted that the upkeep on this place is tremendous, to say the least."

"You make a good point. I suppose it's also perspective, right?"

"Yes. If you have a more positive outlook on life, you

weather the ups and downs. Thanks to some therapy and a great upbringing with our amazing mother, we get knocked down..."

As I knew she would, she sang the line from the Chumbawamba song about getting up again.

I smiled. "Not everyone is like us."

"It's harder some days than others, but you're right. I do wish we knew what happened to our father, though. And I wish Mom knew about our grandfather before she died."

Our father was another mystery we'd yet to solve. Years ago, he went missing while on a military mission. Our grandfather had no idea what had happened, and the government had not responded to his request for information.

We'd also tried to reach out, but our letters had been ignored. I'd handed over the official requests to our lawyer.

Our dad went missing when Mom was pregnant with us. Through a series of mishaps, we believe she thought he'd ghosted her. But in truth, he'd gone missing.

"Me too," I said. "I wish we'd met our grandfather as well. From all the stories, he sounds like he was a great man. I mean, just look at the bookstore he left you. He must have been brilliant to create such a place."

"He left it to us. I just run it," she said. "But it is magical."

"But I guess someone could take all those events in our life and maybe say the family was cursed. In truth, it's life's bumpy road."

She sighed. "Doesn't make it any easier to accept."

"True."

"But we have just as much that's good. We have Mr. Poe, our lovely neighbors, and a beautiful home. We had a mom who loved us and would have done anything for us. She supported our dreams, and we have each other. We're lucky."

I smiled. She'd gone through one of the hardest times of her life, and I loved that she could once again see the world through her prism of positivity.

"We are."

I meant what I said about not believing in curses.

But the priest had been murdered downstairs. His rocky road of life had come to an end. And there was a good chance the killer was still in the castle.

FIVE

When I woke up later that morning, it was nearly ten. After a quick shower and dressing for the chill in the castle, I went in search of my sister and Mr. Poe. I didn't like the idea of them walking around alone while there was a murderer on the loose.

That was if the killer was still here. It was possible they had escaped before the storm hit the night before. If it were me, I would have run away as fast as possible.

Not that I'd commit murder. But I write mysteries and I'm always thinking about ways to get away with murder.

I shivered. It was very different when it was real. Anyone in the castle could have been the murderer.

But it could have been a stranger or one of the staff members.

I wonder if Kieran is still here? I had so many unanswered questions. Maybe they'd been able to pull some fingerprints to help solve the crime. Sister Sarah was still at the top of my list—except she was so petite.

Maybe she works out and has good upper-body strength. Though it was difficult to know under that habit and tunic.

When I turned the corner on the bottom floor my question

about Kieran was answered. He was standing outside the
study, speaking with someone I didn't recognize. The man was
dressed in coveralls and wore a gardening belt around his
waist.

"No, sir," the man said. I stood a few feet away, not wanting
to interrupt but curious as to what he had to say. Kieran's back
was to me, so he hadn't noticed me there.

"And did you see anyone earlier in the day who wasn't a
guest?"

The man shook his head. "We get an agenda with pictures
of the guests so that we know who should be on the property
during the weekends we're open to the public."

I wondered how that worked, and then I remembered
having to scan in our IDs when we made the reservations. At
the time, I'd thought it was a lot of security for a place in the
middle of nowhere. But if the priest's ID had been scanned, that
had to have given Kieran some clue as to who he really was.
Though it was probably fake. Otherwise the O'Sullivans would
have known his real name wasn't Brennen.

"And no one left after the storm started?" Kieran asked.

"The river fills up fast. I live in the cottage just off the main
entrance. I don't see everyone who comes and goes, but I can
hear them. No one left the estate last night. Or if they did, they
were swimming against those currents. You saw how fast it was
going. That would have been dangerous."

Still, it was possible with the loud thunder, he hadn't heard
them, but I shivered all the same. If no one had left, that meant
the killer was still here.

"Did you have a question for him, Mercy?" Kieran asked
without turning around.

How did he know I was there? And then I remembered he
had once told me my perfume was distinctive. I wore Angel. It
was old-school but smelled like sugar cookies to me, and I loved
it. My mom had worn it as well, and it always reminded me of

her. It was a way of always keeping her close. Plus, who didn't want to smell like cookies?

"I'm curious if you'd noticed any strangers in the days before our visit?" I asked. "This place is huge and there are more than a hundred acres of land. It would have been easy for someone to hide out. Maybe they were hiding in an outbuilding."

I'd gone through several scenarios while I'd been in the shower. I think my mind was hoping the killer was long gone and not still with us on the estate.

"Aye, there are a few outbuildings spread out over the acreage," the gardener said. "But the only way onto the estate is through the main gate. Everything is either walled off with nine feet of iron-spiked stone or faces the sea. And the cliffs are too treacherous to climb."

I hadn't realized we were still so close to the sea. Our new home, Shamrock Cove, was a coastal town, but since we'd gone fifteen minutes inland, I'd thought we'd left the sea behind.

I was wrong.

"Right. And you didn't notice anyone coming or going before the rest of us arrived?"

The man shrugged. "I'm usually working around the property during the day, so it's possible someone could have snuck in without being seen. And, yes, we do have outbuildings, but they're checked daily. We store grain and feed for the animals in them, so we have to keep an eye out for wildlife or damp. They're also secured."

"Who has keys?"

He shrugged. "I do, Mr. Gordon and Mrs. Nora. Maybe, a couple of other people. But no one who works for the O'Sullivans would do anything to hurt them. They are the best and take good care of us."

I liked that he was so loyal.

"I'm certain they do. And I'm sure Kieran asked you this,

but did you happen to speak to the priest? Or did you see him speaking with anyone else?"

"No. But I keep my head down and do my work. It's my job to stay out of the guests' way and to be invisible. That said, I need to be gettin' on with it, if you're done with me," he said to Kieran.

The detective glanced at me, and I nodded.

After he left, Kieran stared at me expectantly.

It was all I could do not to laugh.

"Well," he said. "Ask your questions."

"It's like you know me."

He laughed. "That I do. Let's see if I can guess what you were going to ask. Do I have any suspects?"

I nodded.

"There is a house full of them," he said. "No one seems to have heard or seen anything. The last time anyone remembers seeing the priest was on the way back from the whiskey tour."

"Do we still think he's a priest?"

"Sheila took his prints, and I'm waiting for a report. Even though the water has receded some, the internet is still down here, which isn't unusual in rural Ireland. So, she had to take everything back to the station. I'm waiting for her call."

"Did the guests freak out when you interviewed them?"

He chuckled. "A few of them thought it was a murder mystery play. Though, we didn't tell them he was dead. As far as the guests know, the priest is missing. I'm still not certain they're taking things seriously. I'm still checking their alibis for late afternoon. So far, everyone I've spoken to says they were getting ready for the evening activities."

"It should help that half the guests are from the court. Lots of ears and eyes on the others for you."

"True. Gran and the others didn't have many answers, though. The only bit of information that has been consistent is that the priest wasn't the friendliest person."

"That's true. There was just something about him. I'm not even sure I believe he was a priest." I didn't mention that I'd taken a look in his pockets and found an ID. "Was there any identification on him?"

He nodded. "There was. We're checking it out. And we thoroughly searched his room."

"And you still think he is a priest?"

Kieran shrugged.

"What does that mean?" I asked.

"Let's just say his identification and the items in his room made me suspicious."

"Like what?"

"We found a handgun and some papers pertaining to the ownership of the estate here."

"Oh?"

"I should say copies of them. They were old records from a few hundred years ago."

That was interesting. "Did he have a claim to the estate?"

"We're going through the papers. The owners say he was asking a great many questions, but as far as the O'Sullivans are concerned, this place has belonged to their family since the French nobleman built it. From the quick glance that I took last night, that is correct."

"I don't suppose I could look at the papers?"

"They've already gone back to the station with Sheila. But she's making us copies. We're setting up an incident room here in the castle. She'll be back with the originals later."

I pursed my lips. "Well, if he were going to lay a claim to the place, then the owners would be the most likely suspects, right? I mean, Occam's razor: the explanation with the fewest criteria."

He shook his head. "I know what Occam's razor means. We asked for confirmation of ownership, and from what I could see, there is no discrepancy. The place belongs to the O'Sullivans.

There seems to be no question about the validity of their deeds."

"Lots of things can be faked though. Especially with the quality of printers and how easy it is to age paper these days. Anyone with the internet can research how to do that. The priest, for whatever reason, could have forged the papers. I mean, I don't know why. But it could happen."

"Let me guess, it's in one of your books."

"It was. Though in the book, it was the proof of provenance for a piece of art."

"We'll be researching what we were given thoroughly."

I loved doing that kind of research, and it made me wish that the internet was better here. Not that those records would be online, though some would. Especially documents on Ancestry.com where tracking one's heritage could be followed with a step-by-step process. Lizzie and I had been working to track ours since we'd found out about our grandfather and dad.

Other than they were Irish, and some information about the court where our grandfather had lived all of his life, there hadn't been much to find out. According to Lolly, our neighbor, that was because of a great fire in the hall of records in Shamrock Cove hundreds of years ago. But we still searched.

"So, what happens now? Should we head home?"

He shook his head. "I've asked that everyone stay put for the next forty-eight hours. That gives us a chance to go through the evidence, and means we aren't losing any suspects."

"Did anyone argue about that?"

He laughed. "No. That would make them suspicious, though. I'm not certain whoever did this would be dumb enough to call attention to themselves in that regard. That, and another storm is coming in. The only way across the water is by boat. And right now, it's on the other side of the river."

"What makes you think the killer is smart?"

"The position of the letter opener was up and to the right, straight into the major artery."

"So, a professional hit?"

He shrugged. "Or someone who looked it up on the internet. You know how it is these days."

If I ever came up with what I thought was an original murder, I could usually find a how-to on the internet. Nothing was new under the sun. "You make a valid point. Maybe it's smarter to look at the why. The papers seem fishy. I mean, why bring something like that unless he was going to confront the owners?"

"It's a valid question and one that hasn't been answered. Like I said, they have solid proof the place is theirs."

"I wonder if it's tied to the curse somehow." I leaned back against the wall and crossed my arms.

"Don't tell me you believe in curses."

I snorted. "Of course not. But Mrs. O'Sullivan brought it up when all of this happened. Evidently, things have never been easy for the family. They are plagued with tragedies.

"Most people would call that life," I went on. "As we know, it's full of ups and downs. But I think maybe it adds to the drama of owning a castle if you say the inhabitants are cursed in some way."

"Except, the murder didn't happen to one of them," Kieran reminded me.

"True. But something tells me we've only scratched the surface with the O'Sullivans." I yawned. "I don't know about you, but I could really use a cup of coffee."

"On that, we can agree. You've missed breakfast but we've set up in one of the rooms in the front of the house. Mrs. O'Sullivan has provided a never-ending pot of coffee, tea service, and many different types of muffins."

"Show me the way."

. . .

After two cups of coffee, I felt a bit braver. I glanced over at Kieran, who was going through something on his phone.

"Did Sheila send any information yet? And have you talked to Sister Sarah?"

"No to the question about Sheila. And the nun hadn't come down during our first round of questioning. She's the last one we need to talk to. Right now, I'm going through the crime scene photos, so I can write my initial report."

"Can I look at them when you're done? We were in the dark most of the time last night. I might have missed something."

He sighed.

I held up a hand. "I know what you're going to say, but you can't keep me out of it."

"Oh, trust me, I can."

I rolled my eyes. "Yes, but wouldn't it be better if we worked together? You know I can sometimes help with insight from an outsider's point of view. Do we have to play this game every time a case comes up? You have no problem asking for my help when we're talking about your work at the pub."

"That's different," he said without looking up from his phone.

"How so?"

"You aren't involved in those cases and there is no chance a killer might go after you for being nosy. I can't say that here. There's a good chance the killer is still on the premises."

This time I was the one who sighed. "Kieran, you've met me, and I want to help the O'Sullivans. They seem like great people and I hate that this has happened to them."

"You're going to be nosy no matter what I say."

"I prefer the word *interested*."

"Fine. Just don't ask too many questions. Okay? If you feel like you need to be nosy, come tell me. I'll ask the questions."

I nodded, but I wasn't so sure about that. People weren't

always comfortable speaking to the police. Where I was just a harmless mystery writer with way too much curiosity.

While Kieran wrote his report, I went in search of my sister and Mr. Poe. I found them in the large industrial-sized kitchen at the back of the castle.

Mr. Poe was lying at Lizzie's feet, while she listened to Nora O'Sullivan.

Nora clapped her hands together. "Oh, good, Mercy. You've made it just in time for the lesson in making Irish brown bread. Would you like a set-up?" She pointed to the bowls and ingredients in front of the others.

"That's okay. I'll help Lizzie." By help, I meant I would stand there and hand her things if she asked. No one wanted me anywhere near baking. I burned most everything I touched. If it couldn't be stuck in a microwave and heated up, it was beyond my talents.

My sister covered her grin with her hand.

"Irish brown bread doesn't require yeast," Nora said. "You may add whatever you like to the main recipe. But we've kept it to the way our ancestors made it."

She had a patient and kind way about her, and it was difficult to imagine her having anything to do with murdering a priest. I mean, if he was a priest. Everything Kieran had told me left me with even more questions.

"Hand me the buttermilk," my sister whispered. "You're staring at people and you know that makes them uncomfortable."

I had been staring off into space, but when I blinked, I noticed that Nora was looking at me strangely.

"I've never baked bread before," Fiona, the birder, said beside me. "I'm feeling positively domestic." She wore thick, black glasses, and her red hair was piled on her head. She wore a khaki vest with lots of pockets over a flannel shirt and jeans.

"You are doing far better than I ever could," I said.

"When she told us she doesn't spend much time in the kitchen. I told her you could relate," Lizzie added.

I smiled. "It's true, Fiona. I'm glad I'm not the only one."

"Nora promised this was the easiest bread recipe in the world, and it only has five ingredients. And I must admit I ate a quarter of a loaf this morning. I thought it might be fun to learn how to make it."

"Did you come here for birding?" I asked innocently.

"Oh, yes. They have over forty different species here, and those are just the ones that have been identified so far. Yesterday morning I saw a long-eared owl. That was a first for me. They are common in Ireland, but not always easy to find. It was a good day."

She shivered. "Well, except for what happened to that poor priest who is missing. I hope he's not lost somewhere in this weather. Or, worse, drowned."

Oh, he wasn't lost. He'd very much been found. I thought it odd that Kieran didn't want the rest of them to know what had happened. Then again, keeping them guessing probably wasn't so bad and helped the O'Sullivans save face.

"Did you have a chance to speak to him? Or did you see him late yesterday afternoon?"

"I tried to talk to him once. I followed him down to one of the ponds yesterday morning. Well, I'd been heading that way anyway since Gordon had told me they had some early sightings of yellow wagtails and whinchats. And he was right, I saw them both. The trip was worth it just for that." She went off on an explanation of the birds, and I waited patiently for her to finish.

One thing was for certain about Fiona the birder—she was quite passionate about her subject of interest.

"Did he talk to you?"

She shook her head. "I tried. I asked if he was interested in birds since he had binos around his neck."

I assumed binos were short for binoculars.

"But he didn't want to chat. He said he was there for the peace and quiet. Put me in my place. He was beyond rude, even for an Englishman. I'm not a religious person, but I thought clergy were supposed to be kind to their fellow humans."

"Me too," I said. "Not that I know that much about religion." What I did know was from researching the subject for my books.

"How long were you at the pond?"

"Oh, probably two or three hours. They have a grouping of conifers on the north side, where I saw the owl. I took some pictures if you'd like to see them." She bent down and pulled a fancy camera from her knapsack.

I didn't care much about the bird pictures. But then I wondered if it was possible she might have caught something that she hadn't realized.

"I'd love to see them."

She'd gone back to stirring her ingredients together. "Let me get those pictures for you. Just click this arrow on the right when you want to move to the next one. I'm no professional, but I'm quite proud of the quality of some of these. Coming to the castle was an excellent idea. I can't wait to show my friends.

"I told Nora that birders will come in flocks once they see these pictures."

Flocks. I smiled.

If she had killed the priest, she wasn't trying to hide much. I didn't think I'd see much more than birds, but I went through her digital camera roll all the same. As I suspected, most of it was pictures of owls and many different types of birds.

"These are actually quite beautiful," I said.

She smiled shyly. "Thanks. I've sold a few, though only to fund my habit so I can travel the world looking for all kinds of species."

"Now, we're going to shape the loaf," Nora said from the front of the room.

I continued to flip through the pictures, and then stopped at one. Fiona had been taking a picture of what looked like a duck at the far end of the pond. But behind it was the priest and the nun pointing fingers at one another. While their faces were a bit of a blur, their body language spoke volumes. That made Sister Sarah a suspect for sure.

But even more so was the figure who stood at the top of the hill, watching them. The zoom had been on the duck, so everything was blurred in the background, but there was definitely a figure there. Maybe it was just someone passing, but given the circumstances, I would call them suspicious. They seemed to be looking at the pair who were arguing.

I needed to show this to Kieran.

If the nun hadn't killed the priest, it might have been the person in the background of the photo.

Then it hit me. I glanced around the room. All the guests, including our gang from the court, were in attendance. That is, except for one person. It was almost eleven in the morning, and she still hadn't come down.

Sister Sarah was missing.

SIX

After asking if I could borrow Fiona's camera to show something to the police, she agreed.

"Is there something wrong?" she asked.

I smiled. "Oh. No. Nothing like that. I just thought since the priest and Sister Sarah were speaking to one another, the detective might like to see it. That way he can ask her about their conversation. I promise, I'll bring it right back to you."

"Once you shape the loaf, it goes into the pan," Nora said as she instructed the class on how to make the bread.

Fiona waved me away.

I wonder where Sister Sarah is?

I headed back to the incident room. Kieran typed, well, henpecked, his keyboard as he sat at a long wooden table going through some files.

"I feel like someone who is on the computer as much as you, should have great typing skills."

"Are you back to insult my typing, or do you have some information for me?" He pointed toward the camera in my hand. "Did you find your sister?"

I nodded. "She's learning how to make bread with the rest

of the guests, except for the nun. You said she hadn't come down yet, but it's awful late."

"And you didn't want to participate in baking bread?" He ignored my comment about the nun, and laughed after asking the question because he knew my talents were non-existent in the kitchen.

"No. But I was talking to Fiona, who is a birder."

"I spoke with her," he said.

"Right. Well, she mentioned that when she went to the pond yesterday, she tried to speak with the priest, but he wasn't in the mood to talk."

"Right. She told me the same," he said as he flipped through his notebook where he kept his notes on interviews.

"Right. But did she tell you she'd been taking pictures at the pond?"

"Yes. Of birds."

I smiled. "There are a lot of them. But she also caught this." I showed him the picture on her camera.

"That's Sister Sarah and the priest," he said. "We know they were arguing off and on throughout the day. More than one witness has given us that information." Which proved the priest and nun hadn't cared who saw them.

Would it be too obvious if the nun was the killer?

Whatever had been going on with them, they had to be in on it together. And it made sense that she might be the one who killed him. No one else had met him before this weekend, as far as we knew. I kept trying to believe because she was so petite it couldn't be her, but maybe I was wrong. If she was a trained killer, there was no telling what she might have done.

"I saw them arguing, too. But what I'm curious about is who is the person watching them at the top of the hill?"

"It's so blurry, I'm not sure we'll be able to make it out. You're right, though. Whoever it is seems to be facing them."

"That means there may be a third party involved here on

the estate." One more potential killer to worry about. "But you can blow the photo up, right? And don't the police have ways of enhancing pixels? You can clean all this up with one of your machines."

He laughed. "This isn't one of your mysteries, but, yes, we can blow it up. It might at least tell us if we're looking for a man or a woman. As for the pixels, we can send it off to Dublin, but it doesn't work the way you think. The person is little more than a shadow."

"I'm having trouble seeing anyone, besides Sister Sarah, having a motive to kill him. She seems almost too obvious."

"You may be right, which is why we don't jump to conclusions. First, I need Fiona's permission to take the photo from her camera. We have this thing called chain of evidence and I have to go by the book."

I sighed. "Going by the book is boring, but I understand what you're saying. At the very least, we also need to talk to the nun."

He nodded. "If we can find her. I have one of my men looking for her now. He knocked on her door, but she was gone. And she wasn't in the kitchen either, you said?"

"No. But I can help look."

"I think it's best if you don't go out alone. Wait until I can go with you."

I didn't need a man to hold my hand. I was perfectly able to take care of myself.

"But first, I need to ask Fiona for that picture," Kieran said.

"What about the accountant fellow, Maximillian? Have you spoken to him?" I kept meaning to talk to him but the chance hadn't come up.

"Yes."

"That's all I get?"

"Yes."

I rolled my eyes. "Whatever."

He followed me back to the kitchen and spoke with the birder.

"Is everything okay?" Lizzie asked worriedly.

"Yes. I saw something in one of Fiona's pictures I thought Kieran might be interested in and wanted to show him."

She nodded.

Mr. Poe whined and put a paw on her foot.

"What's wrong with him?" I asked. He seldom whined about anything. Though he wasn't so good that he didn't beg for food from time to time.

"At first, I thought he might want some bread, which he is absolutely not getting." She pointed a finger at him. "But he might need a walk. We've been cooped up here most of the morning, and I rushed him earlier so I could get some breakfast before the class."

I turned to find Kieran had gone.

"I'll take him out. I'm not doing anything."

"Are you sure it's safe?" she whispered. "I should come with you."

"No. You wait for your bread to bake. I'll be fine, and I'll stick close to the castle. Besides, you know Mr. Poe will protect me."

She smiled. "Okay, just be careful. Please. I know you're trained to kill a man, but I still worry about you."

She said it like a joke, but she was right. Not long after I'd moved to Manhattan twenty years ago, I'd started taking Krav Maga classes. More to help with my mom's fears of me living alone in a big city than anything else. But over the years, I'd continued my training and added other martial arts.

The detective in my novels was well-versed in protecting herself, so martial arts had become a part of my real life as well. When I discovered I had a stalker, I'd been grateful for that training.

My stalker had been brave enough to break into my apartment and move things around. At the time, I'd just found out how sick my mother was. I believed my mind was playing tricks on me. In hindsight, I knew that wasn't true.

I'd hoped that once Lizzie and I moved to Ireland, all of that would stop. But we'd both felt sometimes like someone might be watching us. We'd never caught anyone in the act, though. We'd almost convinced ourselves we were being paranoid.

But I wasn't so sure.

Mr. Poe barked, bringing my attention back to the present.

After a short jaunt to the pond, I very much wanted to get the lay of the land and check out the hilltop to see if maybe the bystander had left a clue. If he or she smoked, they might have left cigarette butts lying around.

The detective wouldn't appreciate my snooping, but what Kieran didn't know wouldn't hurt him. And Mr. Poe would be there to protect me.

"Come on, boy, time for walkies," I said.

He cocked his head, and I swear there was a look of relief on his almost human face.

I'd barely opened the back door out of the kitchen before he was off at a sheer run. He stopped at the first tree to do his business, and I couldn't help but laugh.

Then he yipped as he waited for me.

"I bet you're glad I showed up when I did."

He yipped again.

"I don't suppose you know which way it is to the pond?"

He stared at me.

"I'm taking that as a no." I pulled the map from my jacket pocket. It was late winter, and I was freezing. Mr. Poe was a water dog, though. He loved the frigid waves and chasing sticks into the ocean. We'd started taking a large towel with us when we walked him down Main Street for that reason. Even if he wasn't chasing a stick, he'd find an excuse to go in the sea. We couldn't keep him out of it.

That was one of his many quirks, but he was an exceptionally good boy for the most part. We had no complaints, and even though we'd had him for only a few months, he was one of us.

I stared down at the map. It was an overcast day, but at least the rain was holding off for now. That said, there were dark clouds rolling in from the west.

"We should probably hurry," I said to Mr. Poe. He barked as if he understood.

The pond was to the east, so we headed that way. It wasn't long until I found myself on the hilltop looking out over it. If I had the picture right in my head, I wasn't far off from where the man had been standing when the photo had been taken.

I searched the area. Since the ground had been trod on by animals, probably one of the hundreds of sheep I'd seen the day before, all I found was churned up mud. If there had been evidence of someone watching the priest and nun, it had long ago been washed away by the rain or destroyed by the animals.

Mr. Poe whined again.

"I have your baggies in my pocket," I said and tried to wave him away. "Take your pick where you want to finish your business. You have plenty of space."

He grabbed the hem of my jeans and tugged with his teeth.

"What's wrong with you?" He tugged again. "Fine, I'll come with you." It wasn't like him to be so anxious. Maybe it was the new place. Or, for a dog, perhaps there was such a thing as too much land, and he was confused.

"Little dude, there is no reason to stress. You can go anywhere you want."

He continued to whine anxiously, and it was then it hit me. That wasn't his I-have-to-poo-whine. It was something quite different.

"Oh. No." My eyes went wide. "Okay, what do you need to show me?"

Even though my wellies were waterproof, the closer we came to the pond, the muddier they became.

"Is there any way you could have chosen a less damp place?" I glanced around, concerned I might see a dead body, but there was nothing but mud and water. Maybe I'd been worrying for nothing and had misinterpreted his signals.

Mr. Poe yipped when he reached the edge of the pond.

"Okay. I'm here. Do your thing."

He ran back to me, and then headed to the pond again.

"Fine." I moved a little closer. That's when the habit came into view. In the dark water, I hadn't been able to see the black fabric until I was much closer.

"What the..." Bile rose in my throat as I raced to the edge of the water. I blew out a breath. The nun was face down and I froze. Then I forced myself to touch her and pulled at her feet until I'd dragged her onto the land. Then I flipped her over and checked for a pulse. I swallowed down the bile that rose again.

"No." I tried to breathe, but my chest was tight.

It was evident from the bluish tinge of her skin, and the vacant stare, that Sister Sarah was very dead.

SEVEN

Kieran stood at the edge of the pond, shaking his head. Since my phone had no signal, I'd run back to the castle to find him. He'd tried to make me stay behind, but I wasn't having it.

"I distinctly remember telling you not to go anywhere alone. What if the killer were still nearby? You could have been hurt."

After gathering evidence, his team was busy bagging the body to take to the coroner.

"First of all, I wasn't alone. Mr. Poe was with me. I was just following him," I said. "I thought he was looking for a spot to do his business. How was I supposed to know he'd found another dead body?"

I shivered. I'd had to wade in almost to the top of my wellies, and water had sloshed inside as I tried to pull the nun from the pond. I was shaking from head to toe, as he put a warm blanket around my shoulders.

A hot bath or shower was definitely in my future.

"And you found her in the water face down?" he asked.

"Yes. Was I supposed to leave her in there? What if she were still alive, or I could have saved her?"

"It's fine. I just need to know for my report. From the looks of things, she'd been dead for several hours. Difficult to know, given the temperature of the water."

Mr. Poe yipped again as if he agreed.

He glanced down at our dog. "I may have to hire you for the force if you keep finding dead bodies."

Mr. Poe yapped like he thought that was a great idea.

I rolled my eyes.

Kieran shook his head but then bent down to pet our very wet dog. "You're a good boy," he said. As always, Mr. Poe soaked up the love.

The detective stood, and then opened his notebook. "Okay, take me through exactly what happened."

I told him about Mr. Poe. "I'm sorry I messed with your crime scene, but I had to make sure she was dead before going to get help."

"I would have done the same. The pathologist said on the phone that the pond has likely washed any DNA evidence off, but we can be hopeful. And we have yours on file so we will be able to write off any of the trace you left on the body."

"I feel bad."

"Well, two people have died, I think that is a normal emotional response."

"Yes, but I meant about suspecting her of murdering Father Brennen or Carl Doyle or whoever he was."

Kieran's head snapped around. "How did you know his real name?"

I swallowed hard. Well, poo. "Before you arrived, I might have glanced through his pockets. Um, to make sure, you know, that he wasn't hiding something." I'd stuck my foot in that one.

"Mercy. You cannot tamper with evidence at a crime scene. How am I supposed to explain your fingerprints?"

"I used a tissue." I gave him my most charming smile.

He shook his head and rolled his eyes. I swear he learned the rolling eyes from me.

"I know. I know. But I wasn't sure when you guys might be able to get there. And I wondered if maybe I might find something that would lead to who murdered him. Like a note. Or maybe he'd stolen something. I didn't know, so I did a preliminary search."

The words sounded lame even to me. The truth was, I was nosy and often stuck my nose into places that it didn't belong. Notably, Kieran's crime scenes. "Have I mentioned, I'm sorry. I'd say I will never do it again, but you've met me. I tend to be impulsively curious when things like this happen."

"You mean murders that put your life in danger?"

I cleared my throat but didn't say anything.

"You are a crime writer, and a darn good one. But you need to leave the investigating and policing to me."

"I do try to do that," I said. "But, like I said, you've met me. I have a natural curiosity and—"

"And you can't help yourself, but it's dangerous."

I sighed. "I hear you." I'd nearly been killed more than once when a murderer had me in their sights. But I'd also helped to solve those cases.

To keep him from yelling at me, I decided to change the subject. "You're going to have a tough time keeping people here with two murders on the property."

"Which is why you won't be saying anything to anyone," he said. "Right now, we're the only ones who know about the nun. The O'Sullivans are aware, and you will say the same thing I told them, which is nothing. 'I don't know' is the only answer I want you to give."

"Okay. I mean, you're here, so they are going to suspect something. Two of the guests will be missing from the various events. I'm not the only one who might be curious about that."

"Then you give the same answer. They are indisposed. I mean it. No questioning my suspects. Got it?"

"Yes. But there have been two murders. That means there is a third suspect, right?"

"How do you know the nun was murdered?" Kieran demanded. "She could have drowned herself."

This time I was the one who was eye-rolling. "In three feet of water? There was petechial hemorrhaging," I said. I had glanced at her neck and seen brown and purple spots on the skin. "She was strangled and left face down in the water. That's odd, right? That the killer has used two different methods? That isn't usually the case.

"And just like the letter opener, strangling takes tremendous strength. She wasn't very large, but still, it isn't easy to crush someone's throat like that. We're looking for a fair-sized man, I'd say."

My mind was already rolling with possible suspects. Mostly of the male variety. I shivered again, and it had nothing to do with the cold. Whoever had done this was knocking people off, and we were stuck on the property with them.

"No one has left, right?"

"The bridge still isn't passable. The only way off the estate is in one of our boats."

I chewed on my lip. "That means the killer is still here."

Kieran sighed. "They're about to serve lunch. Go back to the house and take Mr. Poe with you. You need to warm up before you catch your death."

Mr. Poe yipped as if he were happy to do just that. Even though he liked the frigid ocean waters, he also appreciated being warm and well-fed. We had that in common.

"I guess we aren't wanted," I said, as I pulled the blanket tighter around my shoulders. "Come on, boy."

He followed me back to the house. Since my wellies were covered in mud, I left them in the passage that led outside from the kitchen. I used one of the towels left out for guests to dry off Mr. Poe. Then I put it in the laundry bin provided.

Lizzie was in the kitchen wrapping up a loaf of bread in some cloth.

"Can you give me a slice?" I asked. "I'm starving."

Without missing a beat, she gave me a piece. Then she went to the fridge and pulled out some butter. I slathered it on. I had a fondness for Irish bread, and it was even better just out of the oven.

"Why were you gone for so long and why is Mr. Poe so damp? I thought the rain had paused."

"Mr. Poe ventured a bit too close to the pond."

Her eyes went wide. "Is he okay?" She knelt and scooped him up off the ground. He snuggled into her.

Then she glanced up at me with a worried look. "What really happened? Why is he so wet? Why is your face so white? You've had a shock." She glanced from me to him as if I'd done something to him.

"It's nothing," I said. "I need to go take a quick bath and find my warmer socks. My feet are freezing. Is it almost time for lunch?"

"In a half-hour," she said. Then she cocked her head. Not unlike what Mr. Poe did when he had a question. "You aren't telling me something."

Several people came in at once for which I was grateful.

"Oh, the loaves are done," Nora said.

"I was wrapping mine up," Lizzie said. "I took them out of the oven like you said."

"Aren't you a dear," Nora said. "Well, lunch is ready in thirty, if you want to freshen up. I'll wrap these up for the rest of you. I'm sure you're famished."

I was. All that had been left in the basket in Kieran's makeshift office had been bran muffins. It was the only kind I didn't like. So, I'd missed breakfast. Like Mr. Poe, I wasn't one for missing meals.

"I'll meet you in the dining room," I said. "I need to change and find my other socks. Save me a place at the table."

I raced off before my sister could give me another questioning look. Being twins made it close to impossible to hide things from her.

Lunch was a cottage pie, with buttery mashed potatoes on top. The meat pie was one of my favorite dishes. For dessert Nora's staff brought out Irish cream bundt cake, which I'd never had before. Lizzie asked her for the recipe, for which I was grateful. It was some of the best cake I'd ever eaten.

Every time I asked the other guests what they'd been doing earlier in the morning, my sister gave me a suspicious look.

I needed to stop. If she suspected something was up, so would the others. But everyone had been in the classes that morning. Though, I had no idea when Sister Sarah had died. It could have happened the night before.

Once again, we were back to having a castle full of suspects.

"I've never been on a vacation where I feel like I've learned so much and enjoyed it at the same time," Brenna said. While Rob and Scott knew what had happened to the priest, I'd begged them not to say anything to the rest of our crew. Well, Brenna and Lolly.

"I feel the same way," Rob said. "I love learning new recipes."

"I too am glad we did this," Lolly said. "This will be such a fun listing on our Welcome to Shamrock Cove booklet."

"And it will be a fun place for some of our bigger events," Scott added.

"Wait, so you are all neighbors?" Fiona asked. "I missed that."

"We all live on the court," Lolly said. "A small group of homes in the bailey of yet another castle."

"How fun," she said. Then she peppered us with questions. I glanced at Lizzie, who frowned.

Why was Fiona so interested in us? And was there any chance she could have killed the priest and nun? But why?

After lunch, my sister dragged me to an Irish lace-making class. I'm as good a crafter as I am a cook, which means I'm clumsy and pretty bad at making things. But I loved learning about the history of the lace. Like many times through the ages, crafting was how women came to the forefront to help save their families and their nations. Though this contribution was often lost when history was recorded.

"During the potato blight in 1845, women were encouraged to make Irish lace crochet to sell locally and abroad," said Nora. "The income helped to save many families and was even promoted by Irish aristocrats to help those in need. Lady Arabella Denny used her social and political connections to help create the industry that we still know today."

The crochet hook felt wobbly in my hand, and I kept pulling the linen thread too tight. Part of it was my inability to do anything remotely crafty, but my mind was also on the deaths of the nun and the priest.

I'd managed to avoid any questions at lunch by stuffing food in my mouth. Though, once in a while, I'd glance up and eye people suspiciously.

No one paid attention to me, as everyone was busy talking about the various classes available throughout the day. The next one was at the distillery where there would be another tasting of different types of whiskey than we'd had the day before.

"Have you seen Sister Sarah today?" Fiona asked. "I'm surprised she's not here for the class. Is she ill? Can you imagine paying all that money for a visit here and having to stay in your room? It's such a waste. I wondered if we should send up some soup or something."

I'm sure my eyes went wide, but I tried to keep a mask of

confusion on my face. "I'm certain they'd ask for whatever they need," I said. Then I dropped the silver hook on the floor.

"Do you think anything is wrong? Did they commit a crime? The police won't say what happened, but I'm guessing, since they are still here asking questions, that it was foul play. It's kind of creepy thinking people of the cloth are up to no good."

"That sounds like a plot from one of my books," I said finally. "You have quite the imagination. Did you know either of them before they arrived at the castle?"

This time Fiona's eyes went wide. "Do you have any idea what is going on?"

I forced a smile. "Uh. No. The police aren't exactly forthcoming." I didn't like lying. Well, I did it for a living when it came to my novels, but I wasn't usually very good at it in the real world. "I was just curious if you knew either one of them. They seemed a bit grouchy for clergy."

She pursed her lips. "I went to a Catholic school in Dublin, I'd say they were normal in that regard."

"Oh?"

She nodded. "The nuns were always very strict, and Father Peter believed in following the rules and the Bible to the letter. After all that, I went a bit crazy when I went to university."

I smiled. "You seem..." I wasn't sure what I was about to say.

"Too nerdy to be wild?" She laughed.

"I would never say that."

She shrugged. "It's true about the nerdiness. But it started when I was studying art history. I had a botanical and animal drawing class. We spent a ton of time outdoors, which was where I discovered my love of birds. I found I liked being out in nature and photographing and drawing wildlife much more than the clubs. But I'd done my fair share of partying on nights and weekends. I burned myself out.

"I know you're a writer. I've read some of your books. But what does your sister do?"

"She owns a bookstore in Shamrock Cove, and she still has her lavender business in Texas. Someone else is running that for her now."

"Oh, I love a good bookstore. I'll have to come check it out."

"What brought you to the castle on this particular weekend?" I asked.

Something passed over her face, and then just as quickly, it was gone. "I think I said before that I'd heard about the birds here. I've already logged several in my book."

As friendly as she had been, she'd turned suspicious when I asked why she was here.

"You have to forgive her if you told her something and she forgot," Lizzie whispered to Fiona. "When she's working on ideas in her head, she tends to forget things."

"That's true," I agreed.

"I could barely get through writing my papers and exams for school, I can't imagine writing an entire book."

"Me either, and she's my twin," Lizzie said. "I'm lucky if I can devise an email without typos. I overheard you went to school in Dublin. Is that where you live?"

Fiona nodded. "I'm the same, and yes. I'm a curator for a museum there."

"Oh, that sounds glamorous," Lizzie said.

The other woman shrugged. "It can be. Mostly, it's a lot of work and searching through archives for the provenance of various pieces."

"This place must be some kind of gold mine for historical artifacts," I said.

Once again, she flinched and quickly recovered.

What was that about? Was she here for more than birds? In reading the brochures for the castle, I'd read that centuries-old art and antiquities were present. "This place must be full of great pieces."

Fiona nodded. "I'm not certain they know how precious some items in their collection are. If they did, they'd have much better security."

"Oh?" I asked.

She nodded. "I always keep an eye out to see if these old places have art from John James Audubon."

I'd learned about art when I'd been in college, but I was no expert. Most of what I'd retained came from writing one of my earlier books which had been about stolen art.

"Oh? I knew about the books with all the pictures. I didn't know he also painted."

"Yes. Though I haven't seen any here, yet. I wish I could draw. I'm hoping to take classes," Fiona said.

"Let's take a look at your progress. Hold up your designs," Nora said.

My sister's and Fiona's looked like works of linen art. Even our neighbors had turned out some beautiful pieces.

Me, not so much.

Mine was just a bunched-up piece of knots. It in no way looked like the beautiful lace we'd been tasked to make.

"Lace-making takes a deft and gentle hand, and I hope you all have an appreciation for the women who helped save their families," Nora said, smiling down at me like I was a sad orphan girl with no talents.

I could write books. That was about it.

"The owners of Inishmore helped many of those living on the estate and in the village of Shamrock Cove by helping to set up trade routes for the lace and whiskey. It is one of the prouder moments of the family's history.

"Now, there is a break before the next class at the distillery. We hope to see you all there."

"Do either of you know what happened to Father Brennen?" Mrs. Airendale, the wife of the American businessman, asked. "The police wouldn't say anything other than he's missing. Did he die? Why won't anyone say anything?"

"I'm sure everything is fine," I lied. I wouldn't have Kieran blaming me for letting the word out about the murders.

I wasn't sure how much longer the detective inspector would be able to keep the deaths under wraps, though. People were more than curious and now the police would be asking more questions about Sister Sarah.

But I understood why Kieran wanted to keep it quiet for as long as possible. Once people found out there had been two murders, they'd be tripping over themselves to get out of this place.

The nun's pale face flashed through my mind. If I hadn't seen the bleeding in her eyes, I wouldn't have thought to look under her coif to find the bruising on her neck. Someone had strangled her and possibly held her underwater.

I shivered.

My sister cocked her head and stared at me strangely. Mr. Poe did the same thing when he was curious about something.

"What is going on?" she whispered. "Something else is wrong. You just went incredibly pale."

"Later," I whispered back. There were far too many people around. No matter what it took, I planned to speak to each and every one of them. Yes, I'd made Kieran a promise. But that didn't mean I couldn't get to know the fellow guests a bit better.

Someone was a killer, and we had to find them before they struck again.

EIGHT

That afternoon was another tasting of the Irish whiskeys the O'Sullivans made. Everyone was in attendance, except of course the priest and nun. The other guests kept asking questions of me, and each other. They were all curious about what might have happened to our religious guests.

We were seated around a large wooden bar in the corner of the distillery. A flight of whiskeys sat in front of us.

"I know there are people around, but you have got to tell me what is going on. I haven't seen you this tense in months," Lizzie said.

My sister knew me better than anyone else in the world, and she was my twin. There was no way I could hide any of this for much longer.

I shrugged.

Her eyes narrowed. "You will tell me what is happening when we get back to our room."

One thing was certain, someone was determined to sabotage the opening weekend of the castle. But was it only to hurt the O'Sullivans? Or had the killer been after the priest and nun specifically? Or was it about something in the castle? I had far too many questions, and not one of the guests seemed to know them prior to the weekend.

"Today, we will be tasting some of our blends," Gordon said. He was so passionate about his whiskeys. "The first is a classic Irish Buck with citrus."

Whiskey and bourbons were my preferred drink, and everything we'd tasted so far was delicious. The Irish Buck was no exception.

He explained the process, but I watched the other guests around the bar.

Could one of them be a killer? I'd asked myself that same question so many times my head hurt. Or maybe it was all the whiskey.

Killers needed motives. So far, everyone I'd spoken with didn't know the victims.

When the tasting was over, the other guests exited the distillery. Lolly and Brenna followed them out. But Lizzie, Rob, and Scott blocked the door.

"You need to tell us what is going on," Lizzie said.

I glanced behind me. "I will, but not here. I swore to Kieran that I would keep things quiet."

"From everyone else, maybe," Scott said. "But not us. We already know about the priest. Is the nun dead as well?"

I nodded.

Lizzie gasped. "Really?"

"Mr. Poe and I found her in the pond this morning." I went on to explain.

"I was so certain she was the one who killed the priest," Scott said. He took off his cap and rubbed his bald head.

"Do they have any idea who is doing this?"

"Not a clue, I don't think. They're still sorting through all the forensics and doing background checks. We just need to keep our eyes open and travel in pairs, okay? Everyone be careful."

"There is something I overheard from that accountant guy, Maximillian," Rob said. "I heard him on the phone talking about a treasure."

"What? Like a real treasure? Are you sure that is what you heard?"

"Yes. He walked away before I could hear more. I was more curious why his cell worked when the rest of us have such spotty reception."

That was a good question.

"Okay. I'll let Kieran know. But promise me you will all be careful."

"We promise," Lizzie said. "Can you do the same?"

I made the sign of the cross over my heart like we used to do when we were children. "I promise."

What Rob had overheard from the accountant was odd. A treasure in the castle? That seemed a bit much. Still, I would explore that idea with Kieran at some point. That is, after doing some research of my own.

Later that night, I was hungry, and Lizzie, Mr. Poe, and I headed downstairs in search of a snack, and to let the dog out for his nightly constitution. The staff had left an array of sweets and sandwiches on the breakfast bar in the kitchen, for those who needed a bite before bed.

With all the walking we'd been doing, and the fact that I don't do lamb, which was what we'd been served for dinner, I was starving. I'd spent the hour and a half after dinner trying to pretend that all was well with my sister, even though she'd peppered me with one question after another. I wasn't sure how much longer I could hold out. I'd told her, Rob, and Scott most of what I knew, but she had a sense I was holding back.

Being a twin had its pitfalls and keeping secrets was one of them.

As we headed down the stairs, my stomach grumbled.

"You really are hungry," Lizzie said.

"The smell of lamb nearly did me in at dinner."

"I don't understand that. You've never been a picky eater."

I shrugged. "I've just never liked it. Like I said, even the smell puts me off. All I can think of is those sweet baby lambs and I'm done in."

"Yuck. When you put it like that..."

"See?"

She nodded. "I can take Mr. Poe out if you want to stay here and eat."

"Nope. From now on we are connected at the hip. Besides, I can eat on the go," I said. I took a paper napkin and loaded a small pork pie on it, along with a sugar cookie. "I meant what I said, we don't go anywhere alone, okay?"

She sighed. "When we get outside, you're going to tell me exactly what has been happening. I know there is more going on than you've admitted to."

There was no way around it. I would have to tell her the truth. We put on wellies by the back door, and grabbed flashlights as there was very little lighting outside.

A light rain had started again, so we grabbed a couple of umbrellas as well.

A stone path circled the long way around the castle, and we followed it. While Mr. Poe sniffed at the ground, Lizzie put a hand on my shoulder.

"Okay, tell me everything."

"Kieran told me I couldn't," I said honestly.

"Right. That's fine with the others, but this is me. Let me in so I can help you."

I sighed. "Well, as I said, Sister Sarah is dead. Again, no clue who the perpetrator might be."

"This place is getting creepier by the minute." She glanced all around as if the killer might be following.

"I know what you mean."

"You didn't say how she was murdered? Was it a letter opener again?"

"No to the letter opener. It looked like she was maybe strangled, or it might have been drowning, or both. I'm hoping once they do a postmortem, Kieran will share the information with me, but as far as I know right now, she's just very dead," I said.

"That's awful. I can't believe you and Mr. Poe found her. Were you scared?"

I sighed. "Yes. But Kieran will kill me if he finds out I said anything to you."

"Well, you didn't say much. I asked you questions, and you answered truthfully. Why would someone want to kill a priest and a nun?"

"Your guess is as good as mine," I said. "Mr. Poe has become quite adept at finding dead bodies. It's a bit scary if you ask me."

As if he agreed, he yapped and then ran toward some conifers by the distillery.

Lizzie shivered. "I'm regretting persuading you to come here," she said. "I thought this would be a good getaway for the both of us. We've been working so hard lately. Now two people are dead, and you've had to deal with dead bodies again. It's awful, for you and them."

I crooked my arm in hers. "Mostly for them. It is not your fault," I said. "I'm glad we are here. Think about it. There are so many rooms in this castle. Who knows how long it would have taken for them to find the priest if it hadn't been for Mr. Poe?"

"Still. You know how nervous I get when there are deaths. What if the murderer is still here?"

"They probably are," I said. "Not to scare you. But the nun had to have been killed in the last twenty-four hours and since then, the road out of here has been blocked by water and then the police."

"You're not making me feel any better."

"Sorry. But it's true. That's why I don't want you going anywhere alone while we're here."

"I'm worried about you being in danger again. Kieran likes you. He would let us go home if you asked him."

"Not without alerting the others staying here. Think about it. His grandmother is here. If he was truly worried about our safety, he would have evacuated her first.

"He thinks as long as we don't ask the wrong person questions, then we should be perfectly safe. And Kieran likes the idea of keeping everyone together for as long as possible. As of right now, no one but us, and our friends, know a murder has been committed. Well, us, and the killer."

"Do you have any suspects?"

"Everyone here who isn't a friend of ours," I said.

"Really?" She gasped.

"My prime suspect in the priest's murder was the nun. He wasn't who he said he was, and now I'm wondering about her. I feel like we may be back to square one."

"Like, maybe they were both here under false pretenses."

"Yes. And he was carrying ID with a different name. I pulled her out of the pond, but she didn't have anything in the pockets of her habit. I wanted to search her room, but Kieran had Sheila box everything up and put it in the incident room here at the castle."

"Let me guess. You want to sneak into the incident room and take a look?"

"Well, yes. You know how my brain works. I can't just let it go. And maybe I'll see something that will help."

"No ego there." She laughed. "I know you sometimes forget but you write fiction. You aren't the detective in your novels."

"As you and Kieran keep reminding me, how can I forget? You know what I mean. A fresh pair of eyes and all of that. It isn't like we haven't been useful in the past."

"Just because you've helped solve a couple of crimes doesn't mean you should do this every time. We don't want to alert the killer we are on to them."

It was difficult for me to explain. Even though I didn't know those who had died, I felt a sort of responsibility because we'd found them. That and the fact that my writer's brain would not let things go. It was the way I was made. I could be a bit obsessive-compulsive in that regard.

"You've grown closer to Kieran, why don't you just ask him if you can look through things?" Lizzie asked.

I sighed. "I did. And I even gave him a picture of someone watching the priest and nun argue. But it was blurry, and there was no way to see who it was."

She shivered again. "You think it was the killer?"

"Possibly. With the nun out of the picture, the murderer has to be either a guest, one of the O'Sullivans, or someone who works at the castle. I can't imagine the O'Sullivans causing themselves this much trouble on opening weekend. But it might be one of the other guests, or someone else who works here. Since the trouble just started this weekend, I'm thinking it might be one of the guests."

"Maybe we should ask Rob and Scott to come with us when we walk Mr. Poe. You know, safety in numbers," Lizzie said.

"It's not a bad idea. Promise me that you'll always have me, or one of our group, with you, inside and outside the castle." The rain started up again, as the clouds covered the moon. We'd walked all the way down the hill toward the distillery.

"I promise. Unlike you, I'm afraid of trouble. I don't run toward it."

There was a weird squeaking sound as we neared the distillery. We stopped and looked at one another.

"You heard it, too?" I whispered.

Even in the darkness, I could see her eyes widen and the frown lines cross her brow.

"We should check it out."

"No," she said. "We should not. We should go back to the castle and tell Kieran that we heard a strange noise. Did you not just hear what I said about running toward trouble?"

Sensing our anxiety, Mr. Poe ran back to Lizzie and put a paw on her foot. It was his signal for her to pick him up.

She did it, I'm sure without thinking. Those two were so emotionally tied it was as if he was human sometimes. He was there to comfort her before she even realized she needed him. We'd both bonded with him, but he was definitely her dog.

I headed toward the doorway of the distillery, which I was certain had been the source of the sound. Why would anyone be out here this late at night?

That is, unless they were up to no good.

"Mercy, stop," my sister called out. "I mean it. Let's go back and get Kieran. There is no need for us to become part of some horror film where the heroine walks toward the danger."

"There are two of us, and I just want to take a quick look inside. Then we can go tell Kieran. For all we know, it could have been the wind that blew the door open to the distillery, and I don't want to trouble him for that."

But my gut, which I trusted, was telling me something else.

"Mercy, I don't like this."

"I promise we'll stay right by the door. I just want to peek in."

"I'm going on the record that I protest."

"It's fine. Everything will be okay. I'm going to open the door a bit more, look inside, and then we'll head back to the castle. Probably whoever was in there last didn't shut it properly. It's starting to rain sideways again. All of that water is going straight into the distillery. The least we can do is shut the door for them."

She sighed, and I didn't wait for her to agree. I headed for the door. It did squeak, which had definitely been the sound we heard.

But when I opened it, I very much wished I hadn't.

NINE

The glow from my flashlight fell onto a body not far from the door. It was a man. I raced in to see if he was alive. He was face down, but I could tell it was Gordon O'Sullivan. There was blood on the floor next to his head, but he had a pulse.

"Is he alive?" Lizzie asked nervously from the doorway.

"Yes. Do you have your cell? Can you call Kieran?"

She pulled it out of her pocket. "No bars."

"Okay. I'm going to stay here to see if I can help Gordon. I need you to be brave and run back to the castle and get Kieran."

"It isn't about being brave. I don't want to leave you alone," she said. "What if the person who hurt him is still here?" She whispered the last bit as if she realized we might not be alone.

"Whoever did this is long gone. I promise you that." I had no way of knowing for certain, but her voice trembled. I was worried about her. "Take Mr. Poe with you. I'll be fine." There was a broken whiskey bottle on the floor near his head. "I need you to hurry. He's lost a lot of blood. I think someone hit him on the head with one of the whiskey bottles. Run, Lizzie."

"Are you sure?"

"Yes. You know I can protect myself. Be careful. Run straight for the castle."

"Okay." She took off.

After taking Gordon's pulse again, and checking for any broken bones, I rolled him over into the recovery position.

"Gordon? It's Mercy. I'm one of the guests here. Can you hear me?"

His breathing seemed fine, but he wasn't waking up.

I took my scarf from around my neck and put it under his head. There was a nasty gash on the side of his head. As if someone had hit him when he walked into the building. The blood had already started to coagulate.

At least, there is that. The blood stopping meant healing may have already begun.

I used my flashlight to see if I could find the lights in the distillery. It took a minute, but I found them. And even with them aglow, there were still a thousand places for someone to hide among the casks and the huge machines Gordon used to distill the whiskey.

I prayed whoever had done this to him was long gone.

I knelt beside him, and held his hand, checking for a pulse every few minutes while I waited.

"Gordon, I don't know if you can hear me, but help is coming. Everything will be all right."

His eyes blinked open and he winced.

"What happened?" His voice was hoarse.

"You have a bump on your head," I said. "Do you remember anything?"

He reached up to touch his head, but I pulled his hand away.

"It's a pretty serious injury, don't touch. You need medical attention and possibly stitches."

He tried to sit up, but I put a hand on his shoulder. "Help is coming. You need to stay still until they can take a look. It's a big bump. And we need to make sure you're not hurt anywhere else."

"I'm fine," he said. But he was extremely pale.

"Do you remember walking in here?"

"I was doing a last check of all the outhouses and the barn. I thought I saw a light in here. And the door was unlocked. I remembered locking it when I went up for tea earlier. I don't remember anything after that."

He tried to sit up again, but his face pulled tight. It was obvious he was in pain.

"Please, until Kieran's men arrive, stay still. We don't want to cause more damage."

"Do you think someone did this to me? Or did I fall?"

I wasn't sure what to say. "From the angle and the way that I found you, I don't think you fell," I said honestly.

"Someone did this to me? Do you think it's the same person who killed the priest and the nun?"

"You heard about the nun?"

"Yes, several of our workers saw the police down at the pond. I understand the big boss wants to keep things quiet, but rumors are going to spread soon if we don't tell everyone the truth."

"You're probably right," I said. "But since none of them can go home at the moment because of the river, I think Kieran is trying to keep things contained. It's possible the killer is the one who hit you."

It wasn't until his eyes widened that I realized I had said that out loud. Oops. Kieran would be angry with me.

I shrugged. "Or, you know, a thief trying to steal some of your delicious whiskey."

Why had they been out here? Had they been searching for something? I'd heard the word treasure earlier. Was that rumor true? I shook it off. It was as likely as the fairy stories we'd heard about Ireland.

"There are hundreds of years of history of the castle and the land around it," I said. "But I'm curious if there is something here that people would be willing to kill for. Or if you keep any sort of records out here that they could have been searching for?"

"What do you mean?"

"Maybe something related to the history of the place or even old bottles of whiskey that might be worth a lot?"

He glanced over at the bottle that was a few inches from his head. "That's one of our newest batch," he said as his eyes tried to focus on it.

"We've lots of old stories. Like most places in Ireland, we have a bloody past going back hundreds of years. But I don't understand why someone is trying to sabotage us now. We live a peaceful life here. And have for as long as I can remember. We may not make much money, but we run a solid business. Someone is against us, though. I'd bet money on it."

"Is that how you see the murders—as sabotage?" Everything I'd been thinking was conjecture. I had no more proof than Gordon did when it came to the why of the crimes.

"What else could it be? Someone wants to give us a bad name. They are killing off our guests. I mean, a priest and a nun. It doesn't get much worse, does it?"

But who would want them to fail?

"I know you've been asked before, but did you know either of them before they came here?" I wasn't willing to share that there was no way the man who was murdered had been a priest. His ID said otherwise. And I had a feeling when I could finally access the internet, I'd have more answers about Sister Sarah as well. Not many nuns had dyed blonde hair. Something that had just hit me while I sat here with Gordon.

And it followed that if the pretend priest knew the fake nun, that they'd both been here for nefarious purposes. Maybe they'd been working together or they were rivals. But it was the third party, the killer, who had me more confused than ever.

"No, we'd never met either of them before," Gordon said, answering my question.

"Did they come together?"

"No. We had a van pick Sister Sarah up at the train station but the priest came in earlier. It's odd, though."

"What is?"

"They acted like they didn't know one another. My wife had a small tea set up for when all the guests arrived. She says one never knows who might be hungry. At the tea, she had the guests introduce themselves to one another. You and your sister weren't here yet."

That had been my fault. I'd forgotten to set my alarm and overslept. Lizzie hadn't been happy with me. She likes being punctual. But to me, time is usually relative since I spend a great deal of it writing stories in my head.

"And what happened?"

"Nothing. They seemed surprised that the other one was here. I can't believe they are dead. Who would do such a thing?"

Someone truly awful. Even if they weren't who they said they were, Gordon was right. No one deserved to die like they had.

Kieran rushed into the distillery with two of his men.

"He's lost quite a bit of blood, but he's conscious," I said, as I moved away.

"I'm fine." Gordon waved them away. "Just need some help up."

"From the pool of blood on the floor, I doubt you're fine," Kieran said. "My men are trained for medical emergencies. Let them check you out."

Gordon sighed but didn't say anything else as the men looked him over.

"What happened?" Kieran asked me, as he helped me up off the floor.

"We were walking Mr. Poe and heard a strange sound coming from the distillery. Lizzie wanted to come get you, but I thought we should check it out first. You know, just to make certain we weren't calling you out for nothing but the wind blowing a door open."

He smirked. "Right." That one word implied he didn't believe I'd even considered asking him for help before I found out what was going on. He'd grown to know me quite well over the last few months.

"Anyway, when I opened the door, I found Gordon on the floor. I was just grateful he was still alive. And I sent Lizzie back to get you. That's it."

"Do you remember seeing anyone else while you were walking Mr. Poe?"

I shook my head. "No. From the way the blood had congealed on Gordon's head, and on the floor, I'd say he'd been lying there for at least a half-hour or more. He said he'd come to check out the distillery because he'd seen a light. When he found the door was open, he went in, but that's the last thing he remembers."

"I see," Kieran said. "Nice, that you've already begun the investigation." His sarcasm screamed loudly.

I ignored him. "Are they back at the castle?" I was surprised Lizzie hadn't followed them back out here.

"Who?"

"My sister and Mr. Poe," I said as if he were daft.

"Sorry, I was thinking. You didn't see anyone else on your walk, you're sure?"

"No, we were quite alone. So, where is my sister?"

"I asked her to stay and keep Mrs. O'Sullivan calm. She was quite frantic and wanted to come with us, but I needed to assess the situation."

"Well, the situation is someone conked Gordon hard on the head. He lost a lot of blood and is probably lucky to still be alive. My guess is he needs to go to a hospital and get some stitches at the very least."

"I don't need a blasted hospital," Gordon said from the floor. "I'm fine."

Kieran sighed and then looked at his men.

"He has a concussion, and the gash is deep," one of them said. "He needs stitches, but we can do that up at the house."

"Shouldn't he go to the hospital?" I asked.

"Safer for him to stay on this side of the river," Kieran said. "It's rising again, and isn't safe for the boats. And the winds are too strong to get a helo here from Dublin."

"I'll not be getting on one of those death traps. You can sew me up good as new here. My wife will tell you, I've a head as hard as stone."

I stifled a smile behind my hand.

A thought hit me hard. "Gordon, is there anyone who is on your staff who maybe would do something like this? Anyone who might be upset with you and Nora for some reason."

"No," he said sharply. "Most of our staff have been with us for years. They are as loyal as they come. They stayed even when we had to cut back on wages a bit. We've given them stock options in the company and hope to make that up to them. They are all as good as they come."

Well, there went that train of thought.

Even though he protested about it, Gordon was loaded on a gurney and wheeled toward the house. They put a plastic rain cover over him. It was coming down hard now. Any sort of footprints would be washed away soon.

More of Kieran's team showed up, I assumed to work on the forensics. After explaining to the wider team what Gordon had said to me, I made my way back to the house. Well, I was escorted by Sheila, his second in command. His last words to me were to not go anywhere alone.

My hands were covered in blood, and I'd left behind the scarf I'd put under Gordon's head. It too had been soaked in blood, and I had no need of it any longer. It would probably be bagged as evidence anyway.

Inside the kitchen, my sister and Mr. Poe waited for me.

"Is he going to be okay? Nora was worried sick about him. They've taken him up to their rooms."

"I don't blame her," I said. "But he was talking and seemed okay when he left. They'll probably need to observe him overnight to keep an eye on the concussion. But I think he'll be all right. He wasn't slurring his words or anything."

"Well, at least there is that." Lizzie wrung her hands nervously. It was one of the many signs she exhibited that the stress was getting to her. "I really want to go home to our little cottage and forget we ever came here. For such a pretty place, it feels so dangerous."

"I don't blame you," I said. But my mind was whirling with possibilities. And I only had one thing in mind. "Why don't you go on to bed?"

I washed my bloodied hands in the sink until the water ran clear.

"Why aren't you coming with me?"

"There's something I want to do first."

She sighed. "Is it something that could get you into trouble?"

"If I don't tell you then you won't be in trouble with me. Nor can you be blamed in any way for helping me do something I probably shouldn't."

"Mercy, leave the detecting to the professionals. Whoever is doing this is serious. That's three people he or she has attacked."

"I am going to be very careful. I'm not going after anyone. I just want to look at some things. You go on up to bed."

"Remember when you said we wouldn't be going anywhere alone? That goes for you as well. Just tell me what you need me to do."

I suppressed a grin.

She might be the more sensible of the two of us, but she was clearly just as curious about what had been going on as I was. While she was usually reluctant when it came to investigating cases, she had my same sense of needing to know things. Maybe not quite to the extent I had, but it was in our DNA.

"Follow me, then," I said.

TEN

The door to the incident room Kieran and his team had set up was unlocked. He must have forgotten to do it in his rush to reach Gordon and me. And yes, if I'd asked, he probably would have allowed me to take a look at his files. He already had earlier in the day, but I only had access to what he wanted me to see.

In his mind, he had to treat us all, including his gran, as suspects. He very much liked going by the book. He was a great detective and didn't need my help, but that had never stopped me from doing a bit of snooping.

"You stay by the door. If you hear anyone coming, let me know."

She rolled her eyes. "I hate being lookout. It's nerve-racking."

"Well, you can go to bed if you want. There's no sense in both of us getting in trouble if he catches us."

"No. I'll do it." She glanced at her fitness watch. "First of all, I'm not leaving you alone for the killer to find you. Don't you think they might have the same idea since the police are busy elsewhere?"

I actually had not thought about that.

"And second, I'm curious as well. But you have exactly ten minutes, no more. Okay?"

I nodded. She'd had a rough year, and I didn't like causing her stress. But something about this case kept nagging at me. I felt like I'd seen something important but hadn't quite put the pieces of the puzzle together yet. My brain was obsessive that way. I had to keep trying until I had a clear picture in my head.

My first stop was Kieran's computer. But it was password protected, and though I had ways of breaking into it that I'd learned from real-life hackers for a book, I didn't have that kind of time. It wasn't like the movies where that sort of thing happened in seconds.

Well, that, and I really wasn't that great at it.

He must have had his black notebook, which he kept everything in, with him because it wasn't anywhere on the long table. It was a shame I couldn't look through it. Sometimes, his detective brain saw things mine didn't.

I searched for more information about the two victims among the papers on the desk, but couldn't find anything. Maybe all of that was at the station, or he had it on his computer.

Bummer. I really wanted to know who the nun was. There had been some kind of bad blood between her and the priest. Hence the arguments. I thought they might have been rivals for whatever it was they'd been trying to find.

But since she'd been murdered as well, and Gordon had been attacked, there was a third party. That person had no qualms about violence, which I had to admit was scary.

There was a box marked Guests. Each of the guests, including Lizzie and me, had a file in there. I was curious about what he had in there about us, but I thought it best to take a look at the others. I was certain my sister and I had not committed murder.

I might think about it for many hours a day when I was writing, but there was no way I could ever cross that threshold to commit the actual act. Well, unless someone hurt Lizzie or Mr. Poe. Then all bets were off. If someone attacked my sister, or our dog, they would be in a world of hurt.

The first file I glanced at was for the accountant Maximillian Herbert. According to the reports he'd been involved in some illegal property schemes in the past, when he was younger.

After learning bookkeeping skills while he was in prison, he'd gone on to become an accountant. How did that even happen? It seemed like there should have been some kind of licensing problem for an ex-felon. Not that I didn't believe in second chances. It just seemed like there would have been someone along the way that said, no, money handling isn't for you.

I wondered if the O'Sullivans were aware their accountant had a record. I certainly would not have trusted my money to the man. One had to be careful in this world when it came to life savings. The last thing the O'Sullivans needed was to fall victim to some scheme to steal their money. They were struggling as it was.

I wasn't certain how to broach the subject with them, but I would. They were good people and deserved to know.

Kieran will kill me.

But I would find a way to work it into a conversation.

There was another file for the Airendales, the American couple. From the notes, it looked as if they'd come to check out Gordon O'Sullivan's business with the intent of possibly importing their Irish whiskey to the States. They owned a liquor distribution company.

Kieran had a note he was waiting to hear back from American law enforcement and Interpol about the couple.

Does he suspect them of something?

As I went through the papers, I found no answers, only more questions.

He had very little about Fiona the birder. He'd printed out the photo from her camera. Even though it had been blown up, it was impossible to see the figure as more than a shadow. It looked like a man, though, it could possibly have been a tall woman in pants.

There wasn't much more about Fiona in the files. She was tall and strong enough to stab the priest, but I just couldn't see her as the murderer. She seemed way more interested in birds than humans. I wasn't even certain she was aware of the other people here. She didn't seem to interact with anyone except my sister, me and the O'Sullivans. She was shy. Not that I hadn't been duped by a woman who murdered before.

We were just as capable as men when it came to committing heinous crimes. But they were usually crimes of passion. That, and few women would be able to strangle someone to death. It took much more strength, and skill, than most people realized.

What we lacked with all of the suspects was motive.

That was except for Maximillian. If he had been involved in a financial scheme with the priest and nun, it would follow that he might knock them off to keep them quiet. Even I had to admit that was a bit of a reach, but he was the only one I'd seen so far who had a record. Did the priest and nun find out about the mishandling of money? Were they possibly blackmailing him? It was as good a theory as any I'd come up with and answered the third-party question.

He went to the top of my list. He had shifty eyes, and more importantly, a crime-filled past. Okay, it had been only one illegal scheme, but that was enough.

At that point I was interrupted. "Your ten minutes are up. Besides, I think I heard someone down the hall," my sister whispered, coming into the room.

After taking quick pictures of the files with my phone, I put the lid back on the box and we scooted out of the incident room.

We'd just turned the corner into the main hall when we heard Kieran speaking. It sounded like he was on his phone. How did he have a signal when the rest of us didn't? Then I saw, he was speaking on a SAT phone that the military used.

"Run a check on the staff. Yes, everyone."

I hadn't seen any files on the staff in the box I'd looked through. He must have had those in a different one. Could the killer be someone who worked here? But why strike now? And why kill the priest and nun? Even though I was sure they weren't clergy, I would always call them that in my head.

While I'm normally good with directions, my mind was busy running through facts on our way to the room. We took a couple of wrong turns but eventually found the way.

"I'm exhausted," Lizzie said.

Mr. Poe yawned so big he almost fell over. It was way past his bedtime. He would sometimes try to drag Lizzie by her pajama legs upstairs if she stayed up late watching television. He was a dog with a schedule.

"Me too," I said honestly. "We've had a lot going on the last twenty-four hours."

"I'd feel safer if Kieran would allow us to go home, but I also want to find out what happened. And I know you'll refuse even if he did let us head back to Shamrock Cove."

"If he lets us leave, he must allow the others to go too. He's smart trying to keep everyone contained, even though it may feel a bit scary for us."

"A bit?"

She shivered.

"Okay, a lot scary. But it is smart. I need a shower. Why don't you go on to bed?"

As I stood under the hot water, my mind whirled with facts like a bingo cage with too many numbers. Except for our lovely neighbors, I considered everyone in the castle a suspect.

But I'd already made a wrong turn. Since most of the staff had been with the O'Sullivans for years, they hadn't been on my radar. That was a rookie mistake. But there was no way I could interview all of them without looking highly suspicious.

Still, from experience, I knew people here in Ireland liked a bit of gossip. Lolly had once said it came from their rich heritage of storytelling. I believed her. All of our neighbors were great storytellers.

In Shamrock Cove, everyone knew your business, sometimes before you did. It was one of the town's many quirks.

Someone in this castle had seen something. Maybe they didn't even understand what they'd seen at the time, but we would figure it out. I had a plan for tomorrow. One that involved a few of my closest friends.

I only hoped they didn't mind being a part of my Scooby-Doo gang once again.

A hand shook my shoulder, and I sat straight up in bed gasping.

"It's me," Lizzie whispered.

She was lucky she'd spoken, as I'd already been reaching out to twist her wrist painfully in a Krav Maga move I'd learned years ago.

"You scared me," I said.

"I heard a noise," she said, still speaking under her breath. "Well, Mr. Poe did, and woke me up. But then I heard it."

I blinked in the darkness and then reached for the lamp. "What time is it?"

"Three a.m.," she said. She waved a hand at me. "Listen."

There was nothing for more than a minute and then there was a strange thudding sound in the wall behind our headboards.

"That," she whispered.

Mr. Poe growled.

I hadn't minded her waking me up. I'd been dreaming a killer was chasing me through the halls of the castle. When I was working on one of my mysteries, that was the kind of dream, or rather nightmare, that was commonplace.

"The place is hundreds of years old, and there is no telling when the plumbing was last replaced. That's all it is."

She shook her head. "No. There's a difference. Plumbing doesn't sound like footsteps. And we definitely heard that."

I was about to ask if she was certain she hadn't been dreaming, when there was a shuffling sound in the wall.

She was quiet, and we sat there for another few minutes. There were more footsteps and it sounded like they were just on the other side of the headboard. I jumped out of bed and unlocked the bedroom door. The hallway was lit with sconces but there was no one out there. Besides, it was the interior wall where we'd heard the footsteps.

Were there secret passages in the castle? It wouldn't have been the first time a family had done that. Throughout history, nobles had to have escape routes built in for when times went south. At least, that was what I'd read. They'd have secret rooms, and access to places where the enemy couldn't find them.

We sat there for another half-hour but didn't hear anything else.

I moved around the room, knocking on walls, trying to find a secret doorway, but to no avail.

Tiredness swept through me, and I yawned. "We'll look again in the daylight," I said. "And if the O'Sullivans aren't around for us to ask questions, we'll see what we can find on the history of the architecture of the place."

Lizzie frowned.

"What is it?"

"Isn't that what the priest was researching before he died? The books on the desk were all on architecture."

Darn. I'd forgotten about that.

"Right, we'll keep this between us. We'll do a bit of exploring tomorrow. And I'll ask Kieran's permission to look at the books on the desk where the priest was killed."

She shivered again. "I really want to figure out who's doing this and go home."

I didn't blame her. This case just kept getting creepier.

ELEVEN

Around eight the next morning, someone woke me by knocking on the door. I sat up, confused about where I was for a few seconds. I'd gone to sleep listening for more footsteps within the walls.

My sister was already up and dressed, so she answered the knock.

"Morning," Scott said. "I don't know if you heard but Mr. O'Sullivan had an accident last night. He's still resting, but the word is he took a nasty fall. Do you guys think it's connected to the murders? Like, maybe someone was trying to kill him, and Kieran's trying to keep it quiet?"

"Oh," Lizzie said. "Is he okay?" She wasn't a very adept liar, but she was doing a great job of skirting what she knew.

"Lolly says yes. It was a head injury, though. One of Kieran's men was watching him overnight for any signs that he might have a brain bleed. At least, that's what Lolly told me. She's in the kitchen helping the housekeeper with breakfast. She asked us to take Bernard for a walk, and we wondered if Mr. Poe might like to go too."

Our dog yipped by Lizzie's feet. "I think that's a yes," she said. "Are you sure you don't mind?"

"Not at all. The more we walk, the more scones we can eat. Lolly gave them her recipe for the blueberry ones she makes."

"Yum," Lizzie said. "We'll be down soon. His leash is by the back door. I hung it there last night."

"No problem. We'll see you at breakfast."

Mr. Poe followed them out the door.

She laughed as she watched them go down the hallway.

"I know Mr. Poe and Bernard are great friends, but they look like Mutt and Jeff when they are together."

I laughed too. Mr. Poe had reached the fine weight of fifteen pounds. Whereas Bernard, an Irish Wolfhound, was closer to one hundred and fifty. But she was right, they'd become friends from the moment they met.

Bernard went everywhere with Lolly because she had narcolepsy. He was her protector, and at times, would gently nudge her awake. He was quite an amazing dog, much like our Mr. Poe.

Lizzie shut the door. "This gives me more time to cover up the bags under my eyes."

She looked beautiful, as she always did. But there was a bit of blue underneath her eyes.

"Did you not sleep?" I had. Well, after spending an hour staring at the ceiling waiting for more noises, and running through the murders in my head.

"Fitfully," she said. "After what we heard in the walls, I'm just creeped out."

"Speaking of that. I'm going to pretend to do some research after breakfast so I can go through the books in the study. I very much want to read about the history of the castle."

"Isn't it a crime scene?"

I shrugged. "Forensics should be finished with it by now. And I'll ask permission from Kieran."

"Will you tell him why you really want to do the research?" She cocked her head in the same way Mr. Poe did when he was questioning my actions.

"If it makes you feel better. Besides, he needs to know there has to be a secret entrance somewhere, because those footsteps we heard didn't come from the hallway. There may be secret passages built into the castle. That would make it easier for a killer to come and go. It may not even be someone inside the house. If there are secret entrances, any of the guests or staff could be sneaking around."

"Yikes. That does not make me feel any better. You're on your own, though. I don't want to miss the tour the gardener is giving later this morning. He'll not only give a history of the flora and fauna but also tell us about how this has become a natural habitat for several native species of plants that can't be found anywhere else in the world."

She sounded so excited. Gardening was one of her passions. But going to these classes might also give me a chance to talk to some of the other suspects.

"Hmmm. Maybe I'll join you for that one. But first, let me hop in the shower so we can get some breakfast. I'm starving."

"You're always hungry."

I laughed. "True."

About thirty minutes later, we made it to the formal dining room, where breakfast was being served. In addition to Lolly's scones, there were plenty of eggs, smoked bacon, sausages, and a selection of other baked goods. The Irish believed in a hearty breakfast. Possibly, a heart-stopping one, but I was starving.

After filling my plate, I sat down next to Sally Airendale.

"Hi again," she said. "These breakfast buffets are fabulous, don't you think?" Sally wore a deep purple sweater set with black slacks, and a ring of pearls around her neck. She reminded me of those women in *Town & Country* magazine.

"They are," I said.

"The food overall has been so much better than I expected. I mean, I thought they might serve lamb at every meal or something. But have you had the blueberry scones? They are so good. I've given up on watching my figure. I'll just do more steps when I get home."

Her husband, who was sitting next to her, wore a sweater vest over a blue button-down with jeans. Even if Sally weren't wearing what had to be a five-carat wedding ring, possibly larger, they would have exuded wealth.

"I have to agree. Visitors won't go hungry during their stay."

"By the way," she said, "we both love your books. I couldn't believe you were here at the castle. We thought you lived in New York or somewhere else in America. Are you here for research? Is the next book set in a castle?"

"I did live in America for a long time. We just recently made the move to Ireland," I said.

"I can't blame you. This place is gorgeous. Do you live nearby?"

Even though there had been a bit of press about me living in Shamrock Cove during a book event a few months ago, I didn't necessarily like sharing the fact.

"We do. And where are you two from?"

"Tennessee," she said with a drawl. "Just outside of Memphis, that's where our company is."

"And what is it you do?" I played dumb. I'd read about them when I'd peeked into the files Kieran had compiled.

"I distribute fine liquors all over the United States," Alex said. "We're looking at expanding internationally, though."

"What brought you to the castle?"

"We've been talking to Gordon about possibly importing his

Irish whiskey. It's a luxury brand, which fits with our business model."

"Oh?" I knew nothing about that business. Though I was a big fan of whiskey. The tasting tours had been the best part of this trip so far. "Is it tough getting permissions when things come from overseas?"

"Not for my brilliant husband," Sally said as she reached over and patted her husband's hand. She appeared genuinely proud of him. "He has distribution channels already set up all over the world to bring spirits to America. Now, he can use those same channels to open up worldwide distribution for the whiskey."

"Let's not get ahead of ourselves, darling," he said. "She's right though. We're hoping we can use those same distribution avenues to increase our international sales and import the O'Sullivans' whiskey."

"So, how long have you known the O'Sullivans?"

She glanced at her husband. "I don't know. How long have you been talking to him, dear?"

He rubbed his chin. "Well over a year, I think. He wasn't keen on overseas sales at first, but a place like this takes a bundle to run, and we're offering him a good share of the profits if he agrees to our deal. He invited us out here so we could understand the history of the place. My Sally loves traveling, art, and antiquities. This place is quite something."

"Yes, it is," I said.

They appeared to be exactly what they said. And since they'd come over from America, how would they even know the priest and nun?

Just then, there was a bustling at the door, and Nora came in looking tired and a bit unkempt. Her normally flawless white hair was in a messy bun, and her clothes appeared as though she had slept in them.

"Good morning," she said. "I wanted to check in and make sure everyone is doing okay." She sounded a bit nervous.

"We're fine," Lolly said. "How is that husband of yours?"

Nora gave her a tight smile. "Hard-headed as ever. He's supposed be resting after his, uh, fall." She stuttered over the words. "But he insisted on checking on the new lambs this morning. He refuses to do what he's told."

"I'm glad he's okay," I said. "I heard through the grapevine that he had a head injury and that can be scary." Okay, I didn't hear it from the grapevine, but I was trying to throw attention away from me and my sister. Just in case the killer might be in the room.

Nora gave a tight nod. I had a feeling she'd been instructed by Kieran not to say anything about the night before. I glanced around suspiciously at everyone. Maximillian, Fiona, and the Airendales were all in attendance. But they all appeared to be nothing but concerned.

"As I've said since the day we met, he has a hard head. I wanted to let you know that we are back on schedule, and the trip through the gardens will begin at ten thirty. The clootie dumpling class is after lunch. The third whiskey tasting, however, will be after tomorrow's lunch. We are sorry to reschedule, but I didn't want to stress my Gordon any more than necessary. Not that he's listening to me." She rolled her eyes. "I thank you for your patience."

"Any word on the nun who was here?" the accountant, Maximillian, asked. It seemed odd, coming from him, but I suppose all the guests had to be curious.

All of the color ran from Nora's face.

"She is still indisposed," Kieran said from behind Nora. Then he came into the room and loaded a plate with food. Some of his men followed suit, as did Sheila. They sat together at the other end of the table.

"I hope she's okay," Sally said. "Poor woman."

"Probably can't handle her whiskey," her husband said under his breath.

She shoved at his shoulder. "Don't be rude. She is a nun."

Is a nun. She used present tense, which maybe meant she really had no idea what had happened to Sister Sarah, or whoever she was. I couldn't see why this couple from the States might want to kill a nun, and I put them lower on my very short list.

Still on my list alongside the staff and guests were the O'Sullivans, as they could have staged the attack on Gordon. Though, I was at war with that because why would they cause themselves so much notoriety on opening weekend? Still, they knew this place better than anyone else.

"Are you still doing the art history tour?" Sally asked. "You have so many fabulous pieces around the house. I can't wait to hear all about them."

"Yes, first thing tomorrow," Nora said. She blinked as if she'd perhaps forgotten that fact. "I don't have the schedule with me, but I believe after breakfast. Except for the change with the third tasting tour, everything else will remain the same.

"I'll be back to check on you soon," Nora stammered and then took off down the hall as if she couldn't get away fast enough.

"Art history? I missed that in the pamphlet," I said.

"This place is like a museum," Sally said. "I wonder if they even know what they have."

"My wife likes art and shiny things. Sometimes a bit too much." Alex gave her a look that spoke volumes, but I didn't understand what he was trying to say.

She shoved him again. "Don't pay attention to him. He's right, though. So far, I've seen original Turners and several French impressionists. There's even a Jack Butler Yeats piece. And those are just the ones I've noticed. Who knows what else might be hanging around here? They have a small fortune on the walls."

She seemed quite knowledgeable about the art here for someone from Tennessee.

I'm a snob.

I'd encountered that sort of snobbery when I first moved to New York. People there automatically deducted IQ points if one was from anywhere but New York. I'd never had much of a Texas accent, but as soon as people found out where I was from, they looked down on me. It wasn't fair, but it was the way things were.

But when I'd made a remark to Gordon about the artwork, he said it wasn't what it seemed. I'd assumed they were all fakes. I mean, I still did. They could have sold one of those paintings if they'd been real and covered their expenses for years.

"I had no idea," I said. I didn't think it was my business to bring up they might be fakes. "I know about the portraitist John Butler Yeats, and, of course, W.B. Yeats. The latter won a Nobel Prize in Literature." I too had done a bit of research since we'd arrived in Ireland. It had a rich history, if a bloody one.

Well, I didn't know a single country that didn't have its share of bloodshed.

"Right," she said. "But the poet's brother, Jack, was an incredible artist. He was also an Olympic medalist. It was when the Olympics still had art and literature involved in the games. He won a silver medal for one of his paintings. It was the first medal for Ireland, I think. I read about it when we were coming over on the jet."

They had their own jet? They were obviously doing quite well for themselves.

"Interesting. I learn something new every day." I had no idea about the fine arts being a part of the Olympics. I always thought it was about the sports. I was a fan of gymnastics in the summer games and snowboarding and skiing during the winter ones. My sister liked the ice skating, but for some reason, watching people dance on blades made me nervous.

She smiled. "I might have done a lot of research before we arrived. It has more to do with my OCD than anything. I don't like surprises. So, when we go somewhere, I want to know everything about it.

"That and our daughter is an art history major in college. I study up so we can talk about things when she is home. She wanted to come with us, but she's doing an internship at the Met. We're so proud of her."

"I love the Met," I said. "I used to hang out there a lot for inspiration and I saw something new every time I went."

"Oh, she is in heaven."

"She should be. Her expenses are costing us an arm and leg," Alex Airendale said.

"Stop it." Sally pointed a finger at her husband. "You're just as proud as I am. You always like to make a fuss about money."

They seemed so normal. Wealthy, but at least they cared about their kid. That wasn't always the case.

Kieran had sat down across the table from us. He'd just stuffed food in his face, when Maximillian the accountant cleared his throat next to me.

"Are you going to tell us what really happened to the priest and the nun? I heard from some of the household staff that they were murdered."

Everyone around the table gasped, their eyes wide. Lizzie and I glanced at one another knowingly.

I looked around quickly, trying to gauge the reactions, but they all seemed surprised.

"As I mentioned to you yesterday, I cannot comment. It is an ongoing investigation."

"Are they really dead?" Fiona asked. She appeared worried. "We have the right to know if people are dying. Was it foul play? Is there a killer among us?" She dropped her fork as if her fears had just registered in her brain.

"Like I said, we are investigating and we cannot comment."

"But if they are dead, aren't the rest of us in danger?" the accountant said. While his questions seemed suspicious to me, I understood his curiosity. I would want to know as well.

That said, why would he create a detrimental situation for his clients? Bringing up a possible murder did not seem like good business. He worked for the O'Sullivans, and his revelation could harm their business.

For an accountant with a stake in what happened to his clients, he didn't seem to be aware of how damaging his words might be with the other guests.

"No. You're quite safe," Kieran said. "Unless there is something you'd like to share with me, Mr. Herbert? Do you know something I don't? Perhaps you have something to add that will help understand the situation better?" Kieran's eyes narrowed as he stared at the man.

That shut the accountant up. He stared down at his plate.

But again, why had he brought that up in front of all the guests? As the man handling the accounts for the estate, it seemed like he'd want to protect Nora and Gordon. And he'd definitely just thrown them under the bus.

I felt eyes on me, and found my sister, Rob, and Scott staring at me.

Yep. Mr. Accountant was going to the top of our suspect list.

TWELVE

The mist that had hung over the property earlier in the day had dissipated as we gathered at the front of the castle for the garden tour. At least, the rain had held off for a few hours. Though more was expected later in the day. I was here for my sister, who was excited to learn about the flora and fauna. She'd even brought her notebook and phone with her to take pictures.

The Airendales, Maximillian, Fiona and the others had joined us.

While I would never admit it to Lizzie, I was there to find a killer.

"I know some of you have met him, but again, this is Jim Gilley, our wonderful gardener," Nora said as she introduced him. "He's been with us for five years now and has done wonders with cultivating the gardens. He knows so much of the history about the place and how the gardens have developed since the first owners created them. I'll leave you in his care."

The giant of a man gave us a genuine smile that welcomed us.

"I didn't think so many of you would be interested in our

gardens. Does an old man's heart good to see so many of you here." He put a fist against his chest.

He seemed to truly love his work, and I appreciated that. People who loved what they did had a passion for it that was often contagious.

"Right then, today, we'll start in the natural gardens. We've done a fair amount of transplanting over the years since I came, to make each garden more distinctive. In the natural garden, we have everything from primroses and cowslip to wild clary and wood anemones, all of which are native to this area."

We walked for a bit down a stone path. He waved a hand to the left. "This garden is one we created since I arrived. Mrs. O'Sullivan calls it the fairy garden. When the Normans came over to Ireland, they brought many of their own species with them. But Mrs. O'Sullivan wanted an area dedicated to native flora and to the fairies."

My sister was grinning from ear to ear at the mention of fairies. She'd loved finding the fairy doors our grandfather had put into our house and the bookstore. We even had a small fairy garden she kept up under a tree in our backyard. She and Mr. Poe spent most of their time out in the garden. Sometimes working, other times playing.

Jim was well-spoken and took great pride in his work. Sometimes when he glanced our way, I had a feeling he was curious about us. I couldn't quite put my finger on it.

Not that a gardener couldn't be brilliant, but it was the self-assured way he presented himself. As if he were quite used to charming people. I don't know why I found that so odd, but there was something different about him.

By the time we reached the rose garden, even I was into the tour. It was still winter but there were some hardy tea roses blooming through the cold season. At home, the only thing my sister let me touch was the watering hose, and even then, she would supervise. I wasn't the best with any sort of plants.

I'd been so engrossed that I realized I'd forgotten to ask questions of those around us.

Maximillian the accountant was up on the hill talking to someone on his cell phone. It seemed to be quite an animated conversation, and I wondered what it was about.

"Some of the roses are more than four hundred years old, and we take great pride in keeping the various species growing."

Along with my sister, Sally was taking pictures of everything. Her husband appeared bored.

"If you have any questions, I'm happy to answer them," Jim said.

"Where did you work before you came here?" I asked.

His head snapped back as if I'd slapped him. Then his eyes narrowed. "That's a strange question," he said. "Do you want my CV?"

Everyone around us chuckled.

"Sorry," I said. "I didn't mean to sound rude. I'm just curious because you're so knowledgeable about everything here. You remind me more of a professor at a university."

Oh my. That sounded even ruder.

He chuckled, as though he found that the funniest joke ever.

"I've been cultivating gardens since I was a wee one," he said. "My da said to understand the world and our place in it, we must study our environments and the land. We need to respect the natural world if we are to learn from it."

Again, he was very articulate, but I noticed he didn't answer my question.

"I'm just truly impressed by everything you've done here. The grounds are gorgeous."

He nodded. "Thank you. Does anyone else have questions?"

A few people did, and he answered them.

"Now, if you'll follow me, I'll take you back to the house for your next class."

"I wish I had someone like him at home," Sally said. "We have some yard guys, but they haven't trained like him."

"Did he say he was trained? I missed that."

"Well, no. I don't think so. But he certainly knows a lot about the place and its history. I can't wait to get back to the castle and go online. I want to research plants that are native to our area in Tennessee."

"Since when are you into gardening? Other than having flowers for the house," her husband asked. "I thought shopping was your main hobby."

She playfully slapped at his shoulder. "A woman can have more than one creative outlet. Besides, I keep telling you clothes and purses are art forms. Every piece I buy is a piece of art."

He sighed. "Says you."

"Stop. You can't talk. You have your toy trains and military war stuff."

"They aren't toys," he said under his breath. "They are collectibles."

"Same thing," she argued.

"You'll notice the plantings directly around the estate are more colorful," Jim interrupted the bickering couple. "That is Mrs. O'Sullivan's doing. She thought the bright colors would liven up the stone exterior. She designed them so there is color even through our winter months and we use indigenous plants."

Was there anything Nora wasn't good at? She could bake, make lace and was obviously skilled in gardening.

I could write. But that's about where my talents stopped. Well, except, I make a mean cup of coffee. That was something I had to learn when I was a struggling writer because I couldn't afford to go to coffee shops. Now, I owned a machine at home that made the best coffee I'd ever tasted.

And during emergencies, like when our power had gone out, Matt down at the local pub was quite the barista, and they had backup generators. The power grid was something we'd learned to live with in Ireland. A strong wind, and they were aplenty, could knock out parts of our town sometimes for an entire day. It was something that Lolly and Rob, who were on the town's council, were looking in to. They were exploring solar energy, which I thought was brilliant.

As people went through the back door into the kitchen, I waited.

"I want to apologize," I said to Jim. "I wasn't trying to pry. I just meant to say your tour of the gardens felt like a university class with you as the professor. I meant it as a compliment."

He nodded.

"And I was only curious where you'd worked before because I'd like to visit those gardens as well."

He cocked his head and stared at me. "I can't say. They are private estates and my former employers don't want visitors. It isn't like this place where tourists are entertained.

"Now, if you'll excuse me, I need to get back to it." He walked off.

Well, there I go, making friends again. My sister often said I had a way of putting people off. She was the opposite. She made friends wherever she went. Though we were twins, we had different personalities and demeanors. There was a reason I spent most of my time alone with the characters in my head.

I blamed my curious writer's brain, which was always full of questions. It needed a constant influx of information. And yes, I was often too blunt.

I took a few steps toward him. "Wait, I just want to ask you one more thing, please."

He stopped and turned.

"Did you notice anything strange about the priest or nun?"

His eyes narrowed. "Who? Are they guests? Can't say that

I've seen them and why would you care? That said, I didn't know them." Then he took off at a near run toward one of the outbuildings.

The way he'd phrased that made me more curious than ever. I hadn't asked if he knew them. But he was defensive.

Another suspect was added to my list. A priest, a nun, and a gardener. Yes, another beginning of a bad joke. Maybe I was reading too much into his behavior. Maybe he just didn't like nosy folks like me.

I took off my wellies by the back door and slipped on the black Converse I'd left there before our jaunt. I was seated on the bench, tying my shoes, when the accountant pushed through the door.

"I told you stop calling me here," he said. "I don't have any answers for you." He was obviously angry and so focused on the caller, he didn't see me there in the mudroom. He stomped out the back door and I caught what he said before it slammed.

"I told you, if there is treasure, I'll find it. I don't need you calling every five minutes to ask about it. And no, you coming out here would be suspicious. I wish I'd never mentioned the bloody thing to you."

Treasure? That wasn't the first time I'd heard that word. Was some of the art real? Or did he mean like a pirate's booty? And it was then I noticed he was on a walkie-talkie, not his cell. I'd wondered since the reception we'd had earlier had gone away with the new storm.

"I haven't been able to get back in there. I told you someone died in the study. The police have it taped off. We don't even know if what you read is true. I'm doing my best. Now stop calling."

Why would he be after treasure? And if it involved his clients, why wouldn't he just ask them? Or, at the very least, include them in his search.

Because he's up to no good.

I needed to get into that study. I wasn't interested in finding some treasure, but the priest had been up to something in there. Maybe, he too had been searching for the treasure.

I wound my way through the house and bumped into Scott and Rob on my way to the incident room.

"What are you two doing?" I asked.

They put a finger to their lips. Then Scott took my hand and pulled me toward the room where cocktails had been served the first night we'd been there. Then they slid the doors closed.

"What's going on?" I whispered.

"We just saw that woman from the States slipping a porcelain figurine into her coat pocket," Rob said.

"What? Sally? Are you sure?"

"She couldn't see us around the corner," Scott added. "She looked at it for a minute, smiled, and then stuck it in her pocket. Like she owned it. I can't believe she's a thief. It isn't much of a reach from that to killer, right? She and her husband might be the murderers. Maybe, the priest and nun caught her."

I wasn't so sure about that. I couldn't imagine her as a thief, though. Maybe they'd misinterpreted what they saw. But I wasn't about to say that. Nothing annoyed me more than people telling me I hadn't seen something.

"Where is she now?"

"She was heading upstairs when you came down the hallway," Rob said. "We didn't know what to do. Should we have called her out?"

"Well, we need to tell Kieran. That's something for him to handle."

"Do you think she's some kind of klepto?" Rob asked.

The conversation from earlier, came to me. The things her husband said made more sense now. As did the look he'd given her.

"Well, she does like all things shiny, according to her

husband, but he made it sound more like she had a shopping addiction than anything else. I need to talk to Kieran anyway. Why don't you come with me?"

They followed me to the incident room. Kieran was alone and I wondered where his team might be. He was on the phone and held up a finger for us to wait.

We sat down at the table across from him.

After he hung up, he wrote a few things in his notebook. Then he nodded toward us. "What's going on?"

"First, Rob and Scott have something to tell you."

They relayed what they'd told me.

His eyebrow went up. "When did this happen?"

"Five minutes or so ago," Rob said. "A woman like her could afford almost anything she wanted. I mean, she's wearing clothes today that cost more than I'd spend on my wardrobe in a year."

"How do you know that?" Kieran asked.

"Well, I'm a gay man. And when I had my restaurants, we catered to the fashion crowd. I learned a few things back then. Those pearl earrings she wears are from Cartier. Her hair was up yesterday, and I could see the metal tag on the matching necklace. Why would someone with that kind of money steal? It doesn't make sense. She could have whatever she wants."

"If she is a kleptomaniac, it's an illness," I said. "A psychological one. More than likely she can't help herself. The need is a compulsion she can't control. I researched it for two books ago."

"Yes, but she's still a thief," Kieran said. "And you actually saw her put it in her pocket?"

"We did," Scott said. "It was half sticking out of her coat. It was like she didn't care if someone saw it."

"Okay," Kieran said. "Thank you for bringing it to my attention. I'll take care of it. Is that all?"

"I have something to tell you, as well." I glanced at Rob and Scott.

"I think that's our cue to go," Scott said, though he sounded disappointed that I wasn't including them. It was nothing to do with me not wanting to tell them, and everything about my promise to keep my thoughts between Kieran and myself.

"You two, let me know if you see anything else, okay?" Kieran asked.

"We will," Rob said. They rose to leave and stared at me expectantly.

"I'll see you at lunch," I promised.

They nodded, but there was no denying the curiosity in their eyes. They would be peppering me with questions later.

"So, tell me what news you have."

I started with the accountant's phone call.

"A treasure that no one has found in the last hundred years or so, it sounds like something out of one of your books," he said.

"I think I take offense at that," I said. "I wouldn't put anything like that in one of my books." Wait. Maybe I had, in book seventeen. I'd forgotten about that one. No way I'd admit it to Kieran. "I'm just relaying what I overheard. Before you ask if I was following him, I wasn't. I was sitting in the mudroom changing out my shoes. He didn't even notice me there.

"Also, if he works for them, why is he being treated as a guest?"

Kieran sighed. I wasn't sure what that was about. "From what he told me earlier, he came as a guest to understand the full experience."

"Well, he seems sketchy. I mean, you heard him at breakfast. Why would he bring up the idea of murder in front of everyone? Shouldn't he try to help the O'Sullivans save their business? It was almost like he was trying to scare people off."

"Less people around, easier for him to do his treasure hunting," Kieran said.

"Hmm. I hadn't thought about that. Do they know their accountant has a history that put him in jail for property and financial fraud?"

Kieran cocked his head.

Oh. Darn. That was something I'd learned by being sneaky. I'd forgotten.

"And how do you know that?"

I cleared my throat. "I, uh..." I held up my phone. "The internet hasn't been down the whole time."

His eyes did that thing where they narrowed suspiciously.

"Anyway. If he's treasure hunting, that makes sense. He told the person he was talking to that he needed to get into the study. That's where the priest spent most of his time. They have to be searching for something. Maybe they were all working together, and he knocked them off."

"We have no evidence to prove that thought." He was always so sensible when it came to the need for evidence. "I'm going to share something with you, but only because I think you know part of the truth."

I frowned. I had no idea what he was talking about.

"Father Brennen, a.k.a. Carl Doyle, was no priest. For the last fifteen years, he's been in jail for armed robbery."

"Why was he pretending to be a priest?"

"My guess is news of the treasure, or he and his gang were going to rob the place, and it seemed like a good idea to scope it out in disguise. The problem is, from the papers I've seen, most of the art and antiquities were deemed fakes."

"I was thinking earlier if any of the art had been real, why wouldn't the O'Sullivans just sell a couple of pieces to cover their costs? And if there is treasure hiding somewhere, wouldn't they be the first to look for it? That is probably just some rumor."

"I agree with you."

"What about Sister Sarah?"

"She doesn't exist," he said. "She's a phantom. Her finger-prints don't come up on any of our databases. We're pretty sure she was not a real nun. Sheila is digging into that one to see what we can find. But her initial search of orders—a worldwide search, mind you—came up with nothing. It's like she's a ghost."

"Do you think she and the priest were looking for the trea-sure together?"

He shrugged. "And someone killed them both?"

"True. It could have been the accountant since he, too, is looking for it."

"Maybe. I will be questioning him but it's a bit of a reach from white-collar crimes to murder. It would help if we had some idea what they'd all been looking for."

"I need to get into that study," I said.

His eyebrow went up. "Why is that?"

"I feel like the answers are there. Maybe in one of the historical diaries they keep. Have forensics finished in there?"

"They have."

"Can I have the key to do some research?"

"I'll come with you," he said. "But first, you may want to look at box number twelve."

"Why is that?"

"It contains the books that were on the desk when Carl was murdered."

"I can go through these. While you do something else."

"What do you mean?"

I was trying to get him out of the room so I could examine all the boxes, including the ones he didn't want me to see.

"Don't you have a kleptomaniac to confront?"

He sighed. "I do. But if I do that, it means possibly throwing her in jail if the O'Sullivans want to press charges. And, for the moment, I need everyone to stay where they are. At least for the next twenty-four hours."

"Why is that?"

"A few reasons. Once they disperse, it will make it more difficult to follow up with them. And we can't risk letting the killer get away, if he or she hasn't already. That and it gives the pathologist time to give us more information and process DNA."

"Scary that the killer might still be here, but it makes sense. Have you been through Sister Sarah's things?"

He nodded. "Her stuff is in those boxes at the end of the table."

"Do you mind if I go through them?"

"We've been through it and there was nothing of note. Other than she had some jeans one wouldn't normally think a nun might own. There was a Bible and some toiletries. We think the Bible may have just been a part of her costume. Oh, and there is a puzzle box. Maybe, you can figure how to get into it."

"Oh, yes please!" I loved any sort of puzzle.

He waved a hand toward the boxes and then opened his laptop.

The boxes were much like he said. A few items of clothing, a Bible, and some toiletries, including makeup which no nun would be caught dead in, were on the top of the pile. There was also a strange wooden box that looked like something to put jewelry into. Except, it was empty. There was an intricate wooden inlay on the top that slid just a bit when I put my finger on it.

"Huh," I said. I tried to slide some of the other pieces, but they didn't budge.

"What are you looking at?"

"The old-fashioned puzzle box. The one you mentioned. I'd only seen them in movies until we moved into my grandfather's place. He had left a few in the house, and even more in the bookstore. He loved all things to do with puzzles. And so do I."

"Have you found anything in them?"

"Most of the time they contain letters from our grand-mother to him. But we did find a few letters from our father when he was at university. They didn't have their falling out until he was much older.

"That reminds me, I know you've been busy, but has your police search pulled up anything on my dad?"

He shook his head. "You know I would have told you right away. If he's still alive he's either using another name or is completely off the grid."

"And you never found a death certificate?"

"No," he said. "But my request to the military database is still pending."

"So is ours. I know they must get thousands of requests, but the waiting is awful." Lizzie and I had never known our father. Our grandfather had found out about us just before he passed away. He and our father had a falling out, and he never knew what happened to our dad—other than he'd been on a military mission and had never come home.

Lizzie held out hope that maybe he was alive somewhere and perhaps had amnesia. I was a bit more practical and assumed he died on a military mission that they were not going to talk about with civilians. The American government wasn't the only one that kept secrets.

I wasn't some conspiracy theorist. But if someone was on a covert mission, those facts would probably stay hidden. Even if that person went missing.

While Kieran worked on his computer, I sat down across from him and worked on the wooden puzzle box. Every time I thought I'd made progress by shifting one piece, the next one would stump me.

I'd been sitting there for almost an hour, shoving the inlay pieces in different directions, when the bottom part of the box slid open, I jumped. It made a weird scraping sound and Kieran's head popped up.

Inside was a diamond necklace, and a passport.

"Oh. My."

"What is it?" he asked.

I held the passport out to him. "I think I know who Sister Sarah really is and why you couldn't find her."

THIRTEEN

Kieran took the passport from me. The name on the document was Sarah Williams and she wore a face full of makeup and had long blonde hair in the photo. The country of origin was England. So, I'd been right about her not being from Ireland.

I read the information to Kieran, and he typed it into his laptop. There were several beeps coming from the machine.

"Does she have a record?" I asked.

He nodded. "She was the driver in the armed robbery Carl was imprisoned for. But she testified against the others and got a suspended sentence. What I can't figure out is why her prints didn't come up on our initial search."

"That all happened a long time ago. Maybe the fingerprint records haven't been computerized yet."

"Well, if she didn't know about Carl being here, that could be why they were arguing," Kieran said.

"But it's too much of a coincidence that they both just showed up this weekend," I said. "Neither you nor I believe in coincidences."

"True."

"So, do you think he forgave her, and they were working together? They did argue a lot, though."

"It is possible. But we only have conjecture. There is no way to know. Did you ever overhear their conversations?"

I shook my head. "It was obvious they were arguing from their facial expressions and hand gestures, but it was all in whispers. Any time one of us came close to them, they stopped talking.

"Maybe the accountant, Maximillian knocked them off," I said. "I'm just trying to think about the people who are trapped here. I mean, he's very thin but he is the right height to stab up into the heart."

He started typing quickly.

"Are you looking for others related to the heist?"

"I am. But the other two men involved are dead. And they don't look like any of our guests."

I frowned. "So, you were thinking maybe one of them faked his death and changed his name?"

"It happens more than you think with criminals trying to hide their past mistakes."

"You know, in my books, the why of the situation is often the most important question that has to be answered. The motivation of a killer, that is."

"I know what you mean by the why. I'm not an idiot. As you know, it's the same in *actual* police work." His eyebrow went up again.

"Yes. I didn't mean to say it wasn't. I'm just thinking out loud. If that's okay?" The last bit came out with a bit of snark. I never meant to step on his toes. It was just the way my brain worked. I had to say things out loud.

"Okay," he said.

"Why would two people who shouldn't want anything to do with one another show up at a remote castle in Ireland for a long weekend?"

"They were planning a new heist," he said. "With the other two in their group dead, they may have pulled in a third or fourth partner, who's turned on them. But why? We've seen nothing in the castle, or the records, to say that a treasure exists."

"You're right. While there might be rumors of treasure within the walls of the castle, we haven't seen proof of that. But people are weird and greedy. Maybe they know something we don't. I think that tour is first thing tomorrow morning. The art history one. Maybe some of the art is original?"

"I'm assuming you'll be going on that?"

"I will. But what is bothering me is even if Sarah killed Carl, then who killed her? We still have a third party who wanted them dead. And are they still on the grounds?"

"We've had the bridge blocked since we came across the river," he said. "There is no way anyone could have left the premises after the murders. The killer has to still be here. And don't forget, someone knocked Gordon out with a bottle of whiskey last night."

I shivered. "Right. And you've done a thorough check on the staff?"

"We're in the process of it. They have thirty regular staff members on the estate and another ten to fifteen who come in for part-time work."

"That has to be expensive, covering all those wages," I said.

"Yes. I've been going through the paperwork, and it takes millions of pounds each year to cover their expenses. Hence the reason they are looking to expand their whiskey enterprise."

"And why they are bringing in tourists for the weekends." A thought struck me. "Do you think this might be more personal than someone just planning a heist?"

"What do you mean?"

"Well, this is their first soft-open weekend for tourists to stay and do all of the events they have planned. Two murders in one weekend might make potential visitors think twice about coming out here."

"True," he said. "So, you're thinking it may also be some past history between the O'Sullivans and the killer."

I shrugged again. "I mean, it's possible. None of this really adds up. We're missing something. I'm just trying to make different connections for us to explore."

He shook his head. "Mercy, there is no us. I will explore these different avenues with my team. Your job is to stay safe and out of the killer's way. Do you not remember what happened the last time you inserted yourself into an investigation?"

I'd been held at gunpoint and threatened. It was tough to forget that. "I remember. But I will be keeping my eyes open. Besides, I helped you figure out who Sarah really was. It isn't like I'm not useful."

"That's true. You know I appreciate your help."

I smirked. "Just not when I'm too intrusive. There is one thing, though."

"What's that?"

"Like I said earlier, I'd really like to do some research in the study. I think it's significant that Carl was murdered there. He'd been spending time supposedly doing historical research, according to the O'Sullivans. Why? It has to be the treasure, right?"

"As I said before, the books that were on the desk have been gathered for evidence," he said.

He took out a pair of gloves. "Use these. They are in box number twelve over there in the corner."

"I brought my own." I pulled them out of the pocket of my cardigan.

He smirked.

"What are you going to do about Sally Airendale?"

"I texted Sheila at the station, and she's working on processing a search warrant."

"It's the O'Sullivans' property, can't you just ask them?"

"I'm sure she's hidden the figurine somewhere. To go through her personal belongings, we need to go by the book. Until then, please don't say anything."

"I won't. But I will be keeping an eye on her."

"That's not a bad idea. It may be a while before we can get the warrant. Sheila texted and said the judge is on a fishing trip, so he won't be back until tomorrow morning."

I smiled. Small-town justice was quite different from what I'd experienced in New York. Let's just say, it was a bit more relaxed than the big city. Though, in both places everything took longer than one might expect. The city because they were overwhelmed with too many cases. Sometimes autopsies would take weeks, if not months. Things happened a bit faster here, but not by much.

I went through some of the books that had been on the desk. There was a diary of a former noblewoman who had lived in the castle in the seventeen hundreds. The loopy handwriting was sometimes difficult to read, but she spoke in detail about the grand parties that had been held on the estate. There were balls where hundreds of people had been invited.

Her marriage, however, was not exactly happy. Once she'd delivered two sons, her husband had little to do with her. She didn't seem to mind. In fact, he gave her great freedom to travel, which was unusual for a woman of her station. She kept a list of her purchases in her diaries.

She was one of the residents who had acquired many of the pieces of art now adorning the walls of the estate. It was obvious she was an intelligent woman with fantastic taste. She had traveled throughout Europe with her sons. In her words, she wanted them to grow up to be more appreciative of their place in the world, and not a drunken sod like their father.

She pulled no punches when it came to writing about her family and friends.

"This would make a great movie," I whispered. I told him what I'd found so far.

Kieran grunted. "She sounds interesting."

"She is. She was the one who kept the estate going and dealt with those who farmed and lived on the land. From all accounts, she was quite the businesswoman. Even more surprising was that her husband permitted it."

During her time, that simply wasn't allowed. She must have been quite a strong presence.

I took pictures of some of the entries with my phone, the ones where she mentioned her purchases. I wanted to compare them with the inventory list that the O'Sullivans had given Kieran.

Maybe, if the two victims had been after one of the pricier items in the house, we could narrow down why they were here to steal it.

Something niggled at my brain, though. How would they have found out about it? This was an inside job. Someone who lived or worked on the property had to be a part of this.

"Kieran?"

"Yes?" He didn't bother looking up from his computer.

"Do you have someone in mind who might be doing all of this?"

He paused his typing and glanced up at me. "You know I don't make assumptions. As of right now, anyone who doesn't live on the court is a suspect. The pathologist should have a time of death soon. That will help us as well."

"Well, I can narrow it down to a two-hour time span, if that helps. He was on the tour with us for the tasting. Then we all went back to the house, and we found him almost exactly two hours later."

"Right, and during that time, all the suspects say they were either getting ready or were already in the lounge for cocktails."

"But we know there are secret passages all over the house. Anyone could have gone through the walls and back to their rooms without anyone seeing them. Do we think Sarah killed him?"

"Do I want to know how you are aware there are passages all over the house?"

"No. What about Sarah?"

"I told you, I'm not making any assumptions. But she was one of the first to arrive at the cocktails, according to Mrs. O'Sullivan. She fell down the stairs and made quite the scene. What are you thinking?"

"That she was so tiny under those heavy robes. They made her look like she weighed a good thirty pounds more than she did. When I pulled her out of that pond..." I shivered. "She was bony, and I was just wondering if she had the strength to impale Carl with that letter opener. I mean, how sharp was that thing?"

"And if they were working together, why kill him?"

"Well, from what I've learned so far, she was drowned in that pond. The water there is the same as what was found in her lungs and there are some contusions on her neck that showed someone tried to strangle her and she'd then been held down."

"Ugh. That is an awful way to die. I mean, getting stabbed with a letter opener isn't much better. It's the force that I'm wondering about. I mean, your M.E. will know better, but I feel like the killer has to be quite strong. First to get that letter opener up and into the ribs to Carl's heart. And then to hold Sarah down like that. The water wasn't that deep."

I blew out a breath. It felt like I was missing something. There was something in the back of my brain that I'd either seen or heard, but it just wasn't coming to the forefront.

That happened when I was writing sometimes. I didn't call it writer's block when I stalled out a bit anymore. After all these years, I understood it was part of my process for my subconscious to work things out before I could put them on the page. The best thing for me to do was to focus on something else.

"You make a good point. So, our suspect is most likely male."

"And strong," I added.

"That narrows it down a bit."

"The accountant is quite thin and willowy."

"Size doesn't always matter when it comes to murder. When someone is upset about something, they can have unnatural strength. I wouldn't count him out just yet," he said. "Sheila just sent over some files. You were right about his past. And he has current troubles as well, dealing with a partner who has absconded with some of the firm's money. The O'Sullivans weren't victims of that crime, but I'm sure he is also here as a way to reassure them."

"Funny way to handle that by bringing up everything that is going wrong. And searching for treasure. Are you sure he didn't kill his partner and take the money for himself? If not, he's such a negative person I can't imagine why they keep him on. Do you think we should warn them?"

"Not yet. I'll keep an eye on him. From what you just said, he's still looking for the treasure, right?"

"Fair point." If he'd stolen money from his firm, maybe he wouldn't need more.

I wasn't taking him off my list just yet.

Something clicked in my brain. "Oh."

"Oh, what?"

"Well, in my head, I've been thinking the suspects are all guests here. The trouble didn't begin until we all arrived. But as you said there is an entire staff that works here. Anyone could have come in and killed Carl. And Sarah was murdered outside."

"Except we've vetted most of the staff, and everyone checks

out. Again, like you just said, why choose this weekend to start all the trouble? And you sound like you are marking the O'Sullivans off the list, but we don't have any proof that they were not involved."

I pursed my lips. "You're right. Still, I know you don't trust my gut, but I do. It is not them. They wouldn't ruin their chances for this weekend to be successful. This is making my head hurt. And it could be someone from the outside working with someone on the inside. The staff might check out, but do we know everything about them?

"First, I need to get into that study. I want to see what else I can find in there."

"You don't think it's the journals that you just read?"

I shrugged. "It could be one of the things she listed is the treasure they are talking about. I just thought I'd look around while it is light to see if I can find anything else."

"I'll come with you," he said. "I could use a break."

Well, that was a surprise. I was so used to him saying no to my snooping that I just stood there staring at him.

"What?" he asked.

"You said, yes."

He chuckled. "I told you before it was okay. I know I can't keep you from sleuthing, but if you are with me, or your sister, at least we can keep you safe."

I rolled my eyes.

"What is it you really hope to find in the study?"

"In looking at the books that Carl had on the desk, they had one thing in common."

"What's that?"

"They were either inventory lists from past centuries, or diaries. He was looking for something specific."

"Yes, and...?"

"Well, he was still looking, right? I mean, if he'd found what he was looking for, he would have taken it to his room, or it would have been on his person."

"So, you think he was still on the hunt."

I nodded. "And what if it wasn't a painting or vase he was searching for? Or even buried treasure. Though, I'm not ruling that last one out. People can be silly sometimes at the mere hint of treasure. And as we both know, that usually doesn't work out."

"So, what is it you think he was hunting for in the study?"

I smiled. "Follow me, Detective."

FOURTEEN

Kieran unlocked the study and moved the crime scene tape so I could get through. We'd just stepped into the office when there was a strange squeaking sound like a door closing, and then footsteps. We glanced at one another and then Kieran rushed in to check the French doors leading to the outside gardens.

"They're locked." He tried the handles again, to be sure, but they didn't move. And then the sound of footsteps tapered off.

"When did you hear the noises in the walls?"

"Late. After we'd found Gordon in the distillery. There was a thumping sound like a door opening, and then footsteps."

"You may be right about the killer being able to come and go secretly. I'll have the team check to see if there are any clues to the secret walkways once I hear from the owners."

"Well, it might also be a way to hide things. With the police searching the rooms... The thieves could be stuffing things in the walls."

"There is that," he said.

"But the main reason I wanted to come back here is something that just clicked in my brain."

"What's that?"

"Books travel easier than paintings and vases. Specifically, first editions. There are bound to be some here and in the library. They are transportable and can be hidden in luggage. Or, maybe they were looking for some reference to treasure in the house. The thing that is bothering me is how would they know about any of this?"

"Well, we already believe there is a third party who murdered the both of them. Perhaps that person stumbled onto something here. But again, why take advantage now?"

"Revenge," I said. "That's always a good motive. Maybe they had something against the O'Sullivans. I mean I like them both, but have they ever had trouble with the law?"

"No, they're clean," he said. "We checked into them first."

"Oh." I put my hands on my hips. There went that theory.

"Also, I keep saying, why draw attention to the negative side of things if it were the O'Sullivans. What has happened this weekend would only be detrimental to all of their hard work."

"That is a good point," he said. "Dead victims do not help sell tourist weekends."

"Unless people are into true crime," I added. "But I don't think that's what is happening here."

"I agree."

My brain felt like a ping-pong ball bouncing all over the place.

"It's annoying that we only have twenty-four hours of the weekend left and still have so many questions," I said.

"I couldn't agree more. But shall we have a look around? While I don't see criminals like them having much to do with books, that is just an assumption. We might as well check to see if you're right about the first editions."

The bookshelves covered most of the walls in the study. I hadn't exaggerated about the wealth of books in this room. Along with first editions of Irish authors like Oscar Wilde,

Jonathan Swift, and Bram Stoker, there were works by Jane Austen and other famous authors too.

"Everything is alphabetical, and there doesn't seem to be anything missing," I said after an hour or so of looking. "That said, there are several hundred thousand dollars' worth of books on these shelves."

He blew out a breath. "Blimey. Just for books?"

I nodded.

"So, if they were planning to take the books, they hadn't done so yet."

"Right. Though that could be a reach. I mean, most of the books he'd been looking at on the desk had been personal diaries. There is some correlation there, I'm just not sure what. Perhaps Carl was searching for inventory like I mentioned before. Either of the books, or whatever treasure we've heard about."

I pursed my lips.

"What are you thinking?"

"One of the reasons the O'Sullivans have opened up the estate to visitors and have increased their whiskey production is to raise funds to help preserve the castle. I understand them not wanting to part with their treasures and family heirlooms, but just a few of those first editions could help cover their expenses for some time. I mean, there are a lot.

"And before you ask, no, I wouldn't want to part with them if they were in my library, but I don't own an estate that needs so much upkeep. Those books would help keep this place going for a long time."

"But it wouldn't stop the expenses from piling up," he said. "They wanted to create a business that would help keep the estate running for many hundreds of years. Mrs. O'Sullivan mentioned that would be their legacy. That they would not rest on their laurels like their forefathers. Her words, not mine."

"That makes sense," I said. "They seem like very proud

people. And they work hard. Look at how many of the classes and tours they do themselves. Okay. That explains why they wouldn't want to sell off their prized possessions, but that doesn't mean someone else wasn't willing to do exactly that. Are you sure about the household staff? I know I asked before."

"We vetted them and checked their rooms," he said, "and we didn't find anything."

I shrugged. "Anyone who works here would have access. But again, why wait until there are guests here? That's the part that isn't adding up for me. I keep going back to the guests."

Nothing had happened—until we'd arrived. That fact hadn't been lost on me. I felt sorry for the O'Sullivans. They'd put so much work into making this a fun and creative weekend for their guests. When news of the murders got out, it would hurt their business.

Something else clicked in my brain. "When you spoke with the staff, were there any who weren't happy working here? Did any of them seem to have a beef with the owners?"

He flipped through the notebook he always carried. "No. The O'Sullivans received high marks. All the employees seemed to appreciate that they kept them on through tough economic times. Many of them, who lost their homes in the crash, moved into cottages on the estate. They had nothing but respect for the O'Sullivans, which you don't always see these days."

"Very true," I said. "That is admirable. Okay. So, stick with me here. We know there is someone who wanted Carl and Sarah dead. Someone who led them here with the promise of some kind of heist or treasure."

He nodded.

"And we know that someone may be traveling around in the walls. I suggest we check those out as well. If they haven't been used often, they'll probably be dusty and we might find prints." I started going through books and moving them as if they were a lever. When that didn't work, I tried knocking on the back of the shelves to see if there was a hollow area.

"Are you looking for an entrance?"

"Yes."

"We could just ask the O'Sullivans for the plans to the house."

"We could. But the passages might not be shown on them. And I think it's best to keep it to ourselves for now. You're the one who always tells me to keep the circle close."

He laughed.

"What?"

"Most of the time I don't think you listen to me."

I chuckled. "I always listen, Kieran. I'm just not one who follows orders easily. I'm a bit bull-headed that way."

He said something under his breath, and I ignored him.

He started doing the same thing as me, pulling each book to see if something happened, but on the shelves opposite.

It took several minutes, but then I hit a hollow space. I tried pressing in on the shelves, but nothing happened. In movies and television shows, one would pull a book like a lever, and a door would open. I tried doing that with a few volumes, but nothing happened.

"I think I've found something, but how to get into it, I have no idea."

He crossed the room and joined me. The carving around the wooden shelves was intricate, with a lion in the center of each frame.

"Wait. I wonder." I tried pulling the lion's head but couldn't get my fingers around it. My hand slipped and pressed on the figure, and there was a clicking and screeching sound—the same thing we'd heard when we came in and that my sister and I had listened to the night before.

"You've found it," he said.

The shelf moved a bit but didn't open completely. I pushed

harder on the lion's head, and there was another click as something shifted as the door slid aside. The entire bookshelf moved outward, and Kieran helped me pull it open.

I pulled out my phone and turned on the flashlight app. The passageway was dark, and cobwebs clung to the walls.

While I wasn't afraid of spiders, as long as they stayed in their space outside, I wasn't exactly excited to traipse through their domain behind the walls. But my curiosity won out. I took a step, and Kieran pulled me back against his muscled chest.

"What? Is it a spider?" I started what my sister called the spider flap, brushing off my hair and clothes as fast as I could.

He chuckled. "No. Look at the floor."

He let go of me, and I missed the warmth of him behind my back. When had I started thinking of him like that? The notion surprised me, and I hoped he couldn't see the blush on my cheeks. The heat there burned my face with embarrassment.

I liked Kieran in *that* way. I blinked with the shock. But there wasn't time to think about that new revelation.

I stared down at the floor. There were dusty boot prints. The shoe size was fairly large.

"Male?" I asked.

"Or a woman with very large feet. I need to get forensics in here to make copies of the prints."

Part of me was relieved, but mainly I was disappointed. I'd been excited about going into the walls of the castle.

He pulled out his walkie-talkie and ordered his team to the study.

"Okay, I'll be taking it from here, Mercy. Please, do not go searching the estate by yourself."

"I won't," I said. At least, I wouldn't do it alone.

I walked away, needing some air and space. Was there any chance Kieran thought of me the way I did him? We butted heads so often, I doubted it. As far as he was concerned, ours was a professional relationship.

Did I really want it to be more?

I wasn't ready to answer that question.

I went in search of my sister, who was in our room.

"I was wondering where you've been," she said.

"Helping Kieran with some things. You know how we kept hearing footsteps but couldn't figure out where they were coming from?"

Her brow furrowed. "Yes."

"We were right about there being passageways inside the walls of the castle."

She shivered. "That doesn't make me feel great. Do you mean anyone could come in our room without warning?"

"I doubt there are points of entry in every room. That would have made it too easy for enemies to discover the family's hiding places."

"Well, at least there is that."

I told her what I'd been thinking about in the study.

"It figures your brain would go straight for the books. Have you been in the library yet? It's like something out of *Beauty and the Beast*, though on a slightly smaller scale. Floor-to-ceiling books on every wall, except for a few windows that are also surrounded by shelves. It's gorgeous."

"Did you notice the quality of the books?"

"They look well taken care of. I didn't take any off the shelves, though I was tempted. My guess is they probably keep their first editions behind the closed doors of the study. I would. Like our grandfather did too."

In addition to the lovely bookshop our grandfather had left us, there was an amazing hidden library in the cottage. He, too, had many first editions and quite the collection of his favorite authors. It was one of the ways we'd been able to get to know and understand him. And it was obvious our love of books had been genetically passed down. He'd called the room a treasure.

It had taken us a while to figure out that was what he meant by the word, and he was right.

"I'm at a point with all of this that I need you to tell me everything," she said. "My imagination is much worse than anything you could say."

I blew out a breath. "It's just a bunch of supposition for now, but here's what we know so far..."

I explained everything Kieran and I had discussed.

"So do you think it is someone who is trying to hurt the O'Sullivans' business, or something else entirely?"

I shrugged and explained what I'd talked to Kieran about more than once. "It's hard to say. But I think it may be some greedy criminals who do not care who they hurt to get what they want."

"That makes sense."

I told her about the diaries I'd read in the incident room.

"It's too bad you don't do historical fiction. That woman sounds like such an interesting personality. That would make a fantastic movie."

"She was amazing. She basically ran the place and contributed to the wealth of the estate. And I may not write historical fiction, but I could weave her into a current storyline set at a castle. You know, when I finish the two books I already owe my editor."

"I'm surprised she hasn't texted you this weekend."

"One of the bonuses of not having consistent phone signal."

Lizzie laughed.

We'd had a rough year with the deaths in the family, and I'd only started writing again a few months ago. I hadn't quite caught up, but I wasn't as behind as I'd been six months ago. The sheer panic I'd experienced about being able to write had dissipated since we'd arrived in Ireland. The place was good for my soul.

While I'd said I made this move for my sister, it had been

equally good for me. I loved our little village, new friends and neighbors, and living by the Irish Sea. Except for mine and Mr. Poe's habit of finding dead bodies, it had been nearly idyllic.

I opened my mouth to ask her a question but stopped when Mr. Poe growled at the wall.

My sister and I glanced at one another.

"Are you sure there isn't a door to the passageways in here?" she whispered.

Once again, I shrugged.

There was a painting of the Irish countryside on the paneled wall where Mr. Poe sat.

I walked over and pressed on the wall. Nothing happened, but there was a whistle of air coming from somewhere. Remembering the lion in the panel downstairs, I pushed on the decorative trim of the wall panels.

There was a click, and a door popped open.

No one was on the other side, but like the study, there were dusty footprints on the floor. Someone had paused to listen through the wall.

"Well, that's not creepy at all," Lizzie whispered.

"Agreed." I pulled out my cell and turned on the flashlight app.

"What are you doing? Do not go in there. Shut it back up and tell Kieran."

"I will. I promise to tell him everything. I just want to see where it goes. You stay here with Mr. Poe, I won't go far. I only want to see what it looks like down the hallway."

"Mercy, no. What if the killer is in there?"

"They won't be." I didn't know that for sure and my sister knew that. Or at least I hoped not. Mr. Poe was good about knowing when danger was about. But my curiosity won out.

There wasn't much space between the stone walls, and the ceiling was extremely low. Anyone much taller or wider than me would have to bend down and turn sideways to get through the narrow hallways. There was no lighting, only the glow from my phone.

Not sure where it might lead, I moved to the left first. I paused when I heard voices. It was Scott and Rob talking about the rose garden. Scott was going to ask the gardener for some cuttings. He'd already asked for permission from Mrs. O'Sullivan, he said.

Not wanting to intrude on their conversation, I quietly moved down the passage, only to find it closed off by a massive wall.

I went back the other way.

"Did you see anything?"

"No. There is a wall down that way. I'm going the other way now."

"Are you sure you don't want us to come with you?" The dread in her question was quite clear. She wasn't fond of small spaces. Nor was I. But they didn't bother me quite as much.

"No. You two stay here with the door open. I don't know how they open from this side, so I don't want my exit blocked."

"That makes sense. Promise you won't go far."

"I won't." The last thing I wanted to do was worry her, but I didn't like the idea of someone eavesdropping behind the walls. I wouldn't point it out, but the lack of spiderwebs probably meant someone had been up and down this way recently. Though she'd heard the noises the night before.

Had they been listening to our conversations? I shivered.

The passage grew darker as I went away from the lighted entry where my sister stood. Only the light from my phone guided me.

I glanced back and she seemed so far away.

I came to a wall, and the only access was to go to the right. I turned the corner. I could hear voices again, and I paused. It sounded like the Airendales.

"You've been at it again, haven't you?" he said angrily.

"Why? Why are you doing this? Do you understand what could happen if you're caught?"

Her voice was muffled.

Was he confronting her about her klepto habits? Even though I liked a bit of spying, eavesdropping didn't feel right.

Soon enough, Kieran would know what she'd taken once the search warrant went through.

It sounded like Sally might be crying. I felt bad for her. If she did have a psychological problem, her husband should have been more understanding. It wasn't like she could help it.

At the end of the long hallway was a set of stairs that went up another story. I didn't want to worry my sister by staying gone too long, but it was obvious that whoever had been behind the walls had free range to go pretty much wherever they wanted. I didn't like the idea that a killer could come and go as they pleased.

I wouldn't be mentioning that to my sister.

As much as I wanted to continue to explore, I had to get back to her and Mr. Poe.

I turned and headed toward the lighted doorway.

"What did you find?"

"It's pretty extensive," I said. "My guess is this was how they avoided marauders back in the day. They would be able to hide behind the walls for some time."

"I like the idea of the family being able to get away," Lizzie said. "Not so much the idea of someone spying on us."

"Let's move that small desk over this way. At the very least, we can keep them from coming in the doorway."

She helped me move the desk.

Mr. Poe watched us like we were the best thing on dog television. He was a curious little soul. And a dog after my own heart. He was protective of Lizzie and loved us both. He had since the day he came home with us. And while I'd always made a bit of fun about how people treated their pets as humans, we did the same thing with him.

He was a part of our family.

"It's almost time for the clootie dumpling class. Are you coming with me?" Lizzie asked.

"I'll walk you to the kitchen. You know me and baking. We are not friends."

She snorted. "That's true."

"Mean. You could fake it and say my cooking isn't that bad."

She smiled sweetly. "I would. but you're my twin and you can tell when I try to lie."

This time I laughed. "There is that. By the way, what is a clootie dumpling?"

"I think we had one at the pub once. It was like a dessert in a dumpling with raisins and stuff in it. I like the idea of working with recipes that are hundreds of years old. I love that the O'Sullivans are able to do so much in the way of preservation— not just of the grounds and estate but of the routines from the past."

"I don't disagree."

We'd made it downstairs and to the hallway of the kitchen when there was a blood-curdling scream.

FIFTEEN

We didn't hesitate to run toward the scream, which probably says so much about Lizzie and me regarding danger. We would most definitely be killed early on in any horror movie. We ran down the long hallway away from the kitchen and toward the dining room.

Sally Airendale was in hysterics, seated at the table. She shook from head to toe. Her husband had his hands on her shoulders and was whispering to her. Kieran was standing there too, staring at the buffet with a weird look.

"What happened?" I asked, but I didn't wait for an answer. I headed toward the buffet.

Lizzie went straight to Sally and knelt beside her chair. She put her hand on the woman's arm and sat there with her, not saying a word. She's like that, my sister, very intuitive to other's needs. Me, not so much.

It took a minute for my mind to register what Kieran was staring at. There, under a cloche on the buffet table, was a dead animal.

"Is that a raccoon?" I asked. "Are they native to Ireland? I haven't seen one here before."

"Invasive species but not uncommon," he said.

"I'm guessing it's not meant to be an Irish delicacy." It was a terrible joke, but my sense of humor was warped.

"No," he said. But there was a hint of a grin on his face.

"Why would someone put this here?"

"To frighten the guests," he said. "There is no other explanation."

"Someone wants to get them out of the house. But why?"

"So they can continue with whatever they were doing before you and the others arrived."

"But now you are here as well. It seems dumb for the criminals to draw attention to the place by killing the victims."

"Unless those victims were going to give something away," he said.

He had a good point.

Sheila and one of the other officers came in with an evidence kit. They dusted for fingerprints on the cloche.

"I'd like to take my wife to our room," Alex Airendale said. "And we will be leaving shortly. I don't know what is going on here, but we want no part of it."

"You may take her to your room, but everyone will remain on the premises for the next twenty or so hours. If you haven't noticed, it is raining again outside, and the river has flooded and is the only way out of here," Kieran said. "We'll also need to take both of your fingerprints to rule them out."

Alex did not look happy about that fact.

I hadn't noticed the rain, but Kieran was right. It was pouring down in sheets outside. So, once again we were all stuck here whether we wanted to be or not. I had a feeling Kieran had a dual purpose for the fingerprints. He wanted to see if the Airendales had any run-ins with the law.

"Before you go, I have a few questions," Kieran continued.

The other man sighed but then nodded. "What do you want to know?"

"What were you doing in here?"

"They keep tea out for those needing a snack throughout the day," he said. "We came down for a bite before the next class."

"And where were you just before you came in here?"

The other man frowned. "Why would that matter?"

"I'm trying to establish if you saw anyone coming or going from this room before you arrived."

"We were in our room," he said.

I could back that up, as I'd heard them in their room when I'd been snooping. However, I was not about to share that information with Kieran, yet. He wouldn't be happy with me.

"Did someone scream?" Rob asked from the doorway. Scott, Lolly and Brenna were with him. Not long after, Nora came in.

"Is everyone all right?" Nora asked. She stormed over to where I stood with Kieran and Alex. Her eyes went wide when she saw the raccoon, and then she shook her head. "Who would do such a thing?"

"Someone trying to scare the wits out of my wife," Alex said angrily. "Now, if you're finished with us, Detective Inspector, I'd like to look after her." He didn't wait for an answer, taking Sally by the hands and pulling her up from the chair.

Lizzie stepped to the side out of the way.

"Come on, love," he said.

"I want to go home," Sally said.

Alex glanced over at Kieran, who shook his head.

"That's not possible right now. But I've got you. Nothing else is going to happen."

"I'll be sending someone to take those prints shortly," Kieran said.

Once they left, Kieran started peppering everyone with questions.

"Did any of you see someone enter or leave this room?"

"No," Lolly said. "Our group was in the library. They have

some historical documents on display. We weren't anywhere near here."

"Did any of you see someone roaming the halls who maybe didn't seem to fit in with the staff?"

"What do you mean?" I asked.

"Anyone who wasn't wearing one of the gray uniforms."

Again, everyone shook their heads.

"Is it true about the flooding?" I asked.

"Yes," Sheila said as she closed up her kit. "We barely made it back over in the boat. Even with that, it isn't safe right now. It's like a running rapid with all the rocks. It's a wonder the bridge is still standing given how fast the water is rushing over it."

"So, we're trapped with a killer and someone who puts dead animals in a cloche. Yay," Lizzie said. It was the first time someone had said killer out loud, but thankfully, it was just our crew and Nora.

Gallows humor was how we dealt with uneasiness. She'd picked up Mr. Poe and held him tight to her.

"I'm so, so sorry," Nora said. She sat down at the table and put her head in her hands. "I don't understand why this is happening. We've never had any trouble here at Inishmore. My husband and I have lived here for thirty years. He took over when his father died. I mean, we say there is a family curse, and maybe it's not some folktale. I'm beginning to believe it is true.

"Until this weekend, we'd never had any sort of crime, let alone the violent things that have been happening. Who is doing this to us? And why are they so against us doing whatever it takes to protect the estate?"

I sat down next to her. "I'm sure Kieran has asked this more than once, but is there anyone you know of on the staff, or from the outside world, who doesn't agree with what you are doing?"

"No," she said. "And I'm being honest. We have tenants, but they all understand how important this new business venture is, if we are to become sustainable. It's taken years of preparation to get the estate ready for visitors, and they understand how much we need the money to keep going. Many of them have donated hours of labor without charging us.

"I cannot imagine anyone that knows us doing something like this. What are we going to do? Word is going to get out, and we'll be done before we really begin."

I patted her hands, which were in fists on the table. "It'll be okay. When Kieran finds out who is doing this, he'll make it clear in the press that it was an outside party trying to harm your business. Right, Kieran?"

"I can't..."

"Speak on an ongoing investigation," the rest of our crowd finished his sentence. Then we all smiled.

"But you really need to think about your staff," I said. "From what I've seen so far, the person who is doing this has a great knowledge of the inner workings of the estate. They can come and go easily."

"Our staff has been with us for years. I can assure you that they didn't do this. We should have put security cameras in the rooms we were opening. I didn't see any reason for the expense," Nora said. "Now, I wish I'd listened to my husband."

"Why did he think you might need them?" I asked.

"Because we were inviting strangers into our home," she said. "Obviously, he was correct. Do you think it might be one of the guests?" She glanced up at me for the answer.

"I don't know," I said. "Two of the guests are gone. And while I don't know for sure, my mystery writer brain says there had to be a connection between them." At least, Kieran couldn't be mad about me saying that.

"A priest and a nun died on our first weekend. How is that going to look?" She gasped. "I mean..." She stared at Kieran as if he was going to berate her for spilling it had been murder. We'd all been going by the line that the nun was indisposed, and priest was missing.

"Don't worry," Lizzie said. "You're among friends, and we've sort of figured things out on our own. I just said the same thing."

"They didn't just die," I said. "They were killed. My guess is this may have nothing to do with you and your business. Well, at least, not in the way you think."

"What do you mean?"

I glanced back at Kieran. He shook his head and rolled his eyes. "Go ahead. But you are not to discuss any of this with anyone outside this room."

Rob shut the wooden pocket doors into the dining room. Then we all sat down around the table.

I explained my theories about it possibly being one of the guests, but I left out the fact that someone was moving around behind the walls. I didn't mention anything that Kieran had shared with me.

"While I don't know how," I lied, "I think the nun and priest knew one another. They were here at the same time for a reason. I don't believe in coincidences. That they just showed up. I believe someone was looking to settle an old score."

"But why here?" Nora asked.

"Well, that's the big question, right? If we knew that, we might be able to figure out who is behind all of this. But it either has to be one of the other guests, as no one at this table knew the victims. Or it has to be one of your staff." Or, it could be her and Gordon, but I couldn't come up with a motive for them. Until we found out who was doing this, everyone was still a suspect.

She opened her mouth and closed it. "I was about to speak up for our staff, but I don't know what I think any more. Do you have any other ideas as to why they picked our estate for this nasty business?"

"Well, greed is a good motive," I said.

"What do you mean?" Rob asked.

"In the study alone there are hundreds of thousands of dollars' worth of books on the shelves."

Nora frowned. "Are there really? We haven't had the books appraised yet. We were focused on the artwork. It's expensive having the experts come in to do all the appraisals. Our accountant had the art appraised and most of it is fake. We had to have everything appraised for insurance purposes."

Experts. Something jiggled in my brain. Was it possible that one of the appraisers had mentioned something to the killer, the priest, or the nun? Or maybe, one of them had worked for the appraiser? It was a lead at least.

Kieran had moved to the doors and had his notebook open. My guess was he had the same thought. That might explain why they were here, though not why the killer had knocked them off.

"That's understandable," I said. "But I know that you have a lot of money sitting on those shelves, and most likely in your library as well. And this is all conjecture, but what if the priest, nun, and the killer had planned to work together to take some of those things?"

"You have so many, it might have taken a while for you to figure out what was missing. Years even. They would be long gone, and much richer."

"What you're saying makes sense," Lolly said. "But why now?"

"It was the first weekend you had a full tour of guests," I said. "The third party may have been waiting for an opportune time to bring them both here for nefarious purposes. It may have been his or her plan all along to get rid of them and pin the murders on someone else. Perhaps one of the other guests."

"I can't imagine someone out there who hates us so much," Nora said.

"I'm not sure I'd take it that way," I said. "Criminals don't care who they hurt. My guess is this is some greedy revenge plot. At least, that is how it is playing out. Since we have some idea why they are doing this, maybe, we can figure out who it is."

Lizzie shivered. "We may be stuck here but my sister and Kieran will figure it out."

I hoped she was right.

"To be safe, you'll travel in pairs, always," Kieran said. "I don't want any of you roaming the castle without at least one other person with you." He stared pointedly at me.

I may have smirked. And yes, I should have told him about the secret passageway off our room. But I gave myself the excuse that there were too many ears in the room at the moment. I would tell him later.

"And we need to keep our eyes open," I said. "If you see anyone who looks like they aren't a part of the household staff, don't confront them. But do go tell Kieran. Whoever is doing all of this is dangerous."

"That's great advice," Kieran said. "I'd appreciate it if all of you would take it." He looked even more pointedly at me.

"Why the raccoon, though?" Nora asked. "That is pure maliciousness, and it feels directed at Gordon and me."

Hmm. I hadn't thought about that.

Kieran and I stared at one another. There was only one reason why someone would do that.

"A diversion," I whispered.

SIXTEEN

I followed Kieran to the incident room. He went to unlock the door, but it was already hanging slightly ajar. He glanced back at me.

"What?"

"I left it locked. That means someone was in here and unlocked the door."

"Does that mean they had a key? It would have to be the O'Sullivans or the staff, right?"

"Possibly," he said. "They leave the keys hanging in the mudroom, so it isn't like someone else couldn't have picked them up."

"Oh," I said. "Maybe they left some fingerprints behind when they messed with the door," I said.

He nodded. "Sheila, I need forensics," he said over his walkie-talkie.

"Does it look like they took anything or rifled through something?"

"Let me look around," he said.

"Right." I glanced around the room. "The only box that is

open is the one that had Sarah's things in it. Check to see if the diamond necklace and passport are still there."

He put on his gloves and rifled through the box. "The passport is here, but the necklace is gone. Are you sure you put it back?"

"Yes, of course I did. You saw me do it." I'd spent enough time with him to understand that he wasn't implying I took it. Only that I might have put it back in the wrong box. As much as he liked to give me a hard time, we trusted one another.

"What if they also hit up the study? If you give me the keys, I can go check. Or now might be a good time to check the passages in the walls. The killer might still be here."

"No. You aren't going anywhere alone. We'll go together."

"I'm here, sir," one of his men said, appearing in the doorway.

"Dust for fingerprints everywhere," Kieran said. "And check the items in the boxes against the chain of evidence log. I want to make sure nothing else was taken."

"On it, sir."

"And guard the door when you have finished."

"Yes, sir."

"Come on," he said to me. I had to half jog to keep up with his long strides down the hallway. When we reached the study, he pulled out a ring of keys. Once we were inside, we stood in the middle of the room.

"Do you see anything out of sorts?"

I turned in a circle. Everything appeared the same. Except for the shelf directly in front of us. I started to reach for a book that had been put in upside down.

He gently pulled my arm back. "Don't touch. There may be prints." He put on his gloves and opened the book. He was kind enough to show it to me as he turned the pages.

Before the police had arrived the other night, my sister and I had scoped out the study. This whole row of journals had contained nothing but lists of household items dated by year. This one was for 1875.

"It's another log of belongings," I said.

"Why would someone be interested in these old lists?" Kieran asked.

"For the treasure hunt. I know it might sound silly, but I think there is more to all of this than anyone could have imagined. Someone must have learned that there are items worth a great deal here. We talked about that before. But I don't think that's the whole story."

"So, you think that there is buried treasure in the walls or something?"

"Well, we know about the secret passageways."

"Yes, and the walls are all stone. It would be impossible to hide something inside them."

That answered one of my bigger questions about the trail that went behind the study walls. "So do we think that the passageways are just to get secretly from one place to another?"

He nodded.

I went down the row of books to see if anything else was missing. "There aren't any missing, but this is the second time we've seen that these books are of interest. Maybe someone's slowly trying to go through them without drawing attention."

"Except they have committed two murders."

"There is that. And you and the team haven't found any sort of connection between the staff or guests?"

"No. And we've done a thorough search. Though, without the internet, Sheila has been doing the majority of it on her own back at the station. Now, we don't even have that since she can't get across the river until the storm is done."

"What's going on with Sally?"

He checked his phone. "We're still waiting for the search warrant."

"Is it really not enough that people here saw her?" Rob and

Scott were absolutely trustworthy. The pair of them had become solid friends to me and my sister. We considered them, and Brenna, family. They were one of the main reasons living in Shamrock Cove was so much fun for us.

"Yes. But I'll need evidence. And since the rain has returned, no one is going anywhere."

I shivered. "It's weird that we're stuck with a killer."

"It isn't one of your novels, though. I need you to remember that. We are dealing with real deaths, and it isn't safe."

"I know. I promise to be careful. But I need to do that thing where I talk everything out because my brain is trying to tell me something, and I can't quite grasp it."

He nodded. "I feel like we have done nothing but discuss it."

I smiled.

"Okay," I said. "What do we know so far? The murderer had some kind of beef with Carl and Sarah. Carl was a thief, and Sarah had been his getaway driver. We assume they were interested in relieving the poor O'Sullivans of some of their art or antiquities, or finding the treasure, since Carl was hunting through historical documents. And whatever it is, it's enough money that the killer was willing to murder his partners for it.

"To bring them in, the killer had knowledge of what they were looking for. Which means—it's someone here on the estate. I'm sure of it."

That idea I couldn't quite reach came to the forefront of my brain.

"It would have to be someone knowledgeable like the accountant or the gardener. Both of them seem to know about the history of the place. My bet would be Maximillian since we know he has a criminal past. And I hate to say it, but I'm adding the O'Sullivans back in because of the access. Though I don't understand the motive."

"That makes sense," Kieran said. "But you know what I'm going to say next."

"You need evidence not supposition. Maybe, he has one of the journals in his room or something. Can't you do a search?"

"Not without probable cause and a search warrant, which—"

"You have to get from the judge."

"Right."

"Probable cause is you suspect him of murder."

Kieran sighed. "As much as I might agree with you, there are no fingerprints that tie him to any of the crimes. That said, he is a person of interest. We will keep an eye on him.

"Why do you suspect the gardener?" He flipped through his notebook that he always carried with him. "Jim Gilley."

I shrugged. "I don't know really. He knows about the place. He's only worked here for five years but he spoke as if he'd lived here all of his life. Could be that he's just a big history buff, but I found it odd."

"That he was good at his job?" he joked.

"You know what I mean."

As much as he might not like it, I needed to talk with everyone in the house. Even though the place was huge, someone had to have seen something. And maybe the staff didn't feel comfortable talking to the police, but they might be more relaxed talking to me, or better yet, my sister. She and Rob were so affable, and people told them all kinds of things. Lizzie would come home with complete biographies of some of her customers at the bookshop. People opened up to her about their lives and she seldom asked them to.

I wasn't going to learn any more from hanging out with the detective inspector. Well, not at the moment, anyway.

My sister wouldn't like it, but we needed to speak to the staff.

"I'm sure lunch was upsetting for Lizzie. I feel like I should go check on her," I said.

He cocked his head, and stared at me. "What do you know that you're not telling me?"

"Nothing," I said. "My brain is full, and I need time to sort things out. Like you said, you need to find the evidence that links people to the crimes. Maybe they are even working together. Who knows?

"And I want to check on my sister."

"Fine. But be careful and don't question anyone. I don't want you tipping off our killer or putting yourself in danger. Stay away from the suspects we've been discussing."

"Same song, different day."

"I mean it, Mercy. This is serious."

"I'm aware," I said. My writer's brain was at work, though. The priest had been searching for answers. It had to be something to do with the items in this house. More specifically, with treasures. But had he been after a painting or what?

All of the facts floated around in my brain, much like what happened when I was trying to organize my thoughts to write my books. I only hoped they would settle soon and I could figure out the next steps.

At least I had a few solid suspects, even if there was absolutely no proof.

"Where is the next class?" Kieran asked. "I'll walk you to it. I don't want any of the guests going anywhere alone in the castle. I know I've said that before, but I want everyone to understand."

I pulled the schedule out of my pants pocket and unfolded it. "It's the clootie dumpling class."

"My gran makes them best. I'll take you to the kitchen."

. . .

The dumpling-making took some time. I didn't register half of what was being said. I was anxious to talk to some of the others, and the staff. But I had to wait for my sister, who was into the proper way to make the dumplings.

As I have said many times before, the only thing I should be doing in a kitchen is eating. Though, from the ingredients, I didn't think they would be that nice.

They weren't really dumplings at all. The finished result reminded me of bread pudding and was quite tasty.

After the class, Nora excused herself. "I need to check on my Gordon. Please feel free to eat as many of the dumplings as you like."

Most of the guests who attended stayed in the kitchen. We stood around a large marble island.

Brenna and Fiona chatted. Maybe it was my suspicious mind, but I wondered about the birder. She had been at the pond with the priest. Could she be the missing piece of the puzzle?

Motive slapped me across the head. Why? And was she strong enough to push that letter opener through some ribs and into the heart? I didn't think so.

"You seem to be friendly with the police," the accountant said to me. "What do you think is going on? My clients aren't telling me anything. The household staff have said that the priest and the nun were murdered. Is that true?"

You should know since you killed them. I didn't say that out loud, but I was thinking it. I'd warned Kieran he couldn't keep things under wraps forever.

Maximillian sounded genuinely curious, but there was something shifty about him. "How long have you known the O'Sullivans?" I asked, changing the topic.

He blinked and then rubbed his chin. "My father was their advisor before me. So, I guess, most of my life. You've been hanging out with the detective inspector, what can you tell us?"

"She sometimes works as a consultant with the police," my sister said proudly. "But she's not allowed to talk about it."

"I think whoever is doing this has ties to the estate in some way," I said.

"You aren't blaming my clients for anything untoward, are you?" He was abrupt and his tone was rude.

And who said untoward anymore?

"Of course she isn't," Lolly said in my defense. "My grandson is the detective inspector, and I can assure you he has everything in hand. There's no need to worry."

"But they should be telling us something," Sally interjected. "I can't believe someone has been murdered and they won't tell us anything. They should have let us leave earlier. And now we're stuck because of another storm.

"What if it's like some Agatha Christie novel and we're being knocked off one by one?"

Her husband patted her shoulder. "Don't let your imagination run away with you."

"Well, it's not my imagination that something is wonky. And no disrespect to your grandson, Lolly, but people have died here, and I find the whole situation highly suspicious. I don't feel like we're safe. Maybe we should hire a helicopter since we can't pass over the river."

"They can't fly in weather like this," her husband said. "I told you that earlier. Do you see the trees bending outside?"

Oh.

The walls were so thick that they blocked most of the sound from outside. But the winds coming off the sea were blustery.

"You seem in a hurry to leave," I said. "Are you sure it isn't something else bothering you?"

Rob and Scott hid their chuckles behind their hands. My sister poked me in the side.

"What do you mean by that?" Sally asked.

I'd stepped into that. "Nothing," I said. I don't think anyone believed me. I stopped myself from putting my foot in my mouth, but I didn't like the idea that she played the innocent when we knew she was stealing from the O'Sullivans. And, yes, I realized she had a psychological problem she couldn't control, but it was her attitude that upset me.

"Maximillian, since you've known the family longer than any of us, do you think someone is trying to rip them off in some way?" I stared pointedly at Sally. I held her gaze for a bit, and then she stared down at the floor.

"I do not know why," he said. "Most of the art and antiquities are fake. We're in the middle of nowhere. It isn't like someone can just walk out the door with a fake painting."

The way he said it made me believe he'd thought about doing that more than once. There was something about the way he said "fake" that made me suspicious. This guy was up to something, but what? And would he have killed for it?

Then it was like a gong going off in my brain. What if the evidence was in someone's car? The police had thoroughly searched the house and behind the walls. Except for some footprints, at least from what I read in the evidence room, they hadn't found anything out of sorts. But I wasn't sure they'd searched the cars yet.

"When did the family decide to make the estate a money-making enterprise?" I asked the accountant, turning attention away from my foot-in-mouth-disease and trying to cover my blunder with Sally.

"Oh, this is something they've been working on for more than a decade. The whiskey has never been out of production. As that business picked up under Gordon's management, they started investing in the castle. If you're wondering if they are wealthy, they are not. They put everything they have into preserving this place.

"I tried to tell them it was a bad investment. There is always something going wrong, from the plumbing to the electrics.

Since they married decades ago, Nora had it in her mind to open the house to the public. It may be the only thing that saves them. Except now someone has died, which is a disaster for publicity. They'll never make a go of it now."

"Is that true?" Rob asked.

"What do you mean?" Maximillian asked.

"I don't know, we live in a world that is obsessed with murder and true crime."

Sally shivered. "Every time someone says murder I want to hide under the covers," she said.

"What I mean is, there are so many people who love ghost stories that the possibility of being in danger will probably have a big appeal. I mean, it would for me. I love taking haunted ghost tours and such. Or like how the O'Sullivans say their family is cursed. That sort of thing appeals to a lot of visitors. Some people are into history and some like a good scare."

"I hadn't thought about it that way," Maximillian said. "You may be on to something there. There may be a way to spin this weekend that could help them out. Not that they listen to me." He said that last bit under his breath.

It hit me that maybe what I'd been seeing in him was more a lack of confidence. He was trying too hard, and he didn't have his clients' respect.

From all of my research, I understood money was often a motive for murder.

But was his tie to the victims enough for him to kill out of revenge?

SEVENTEEN

That night I begged off dinner. I'd planned to do some snooping and I didn't want my sister or Kieran to worry. Though, if I got lost behind the walls of the castle, I was going to be super mad at myself. I'd thought I might take Mr. Poe with me for safety, but that would have made Lizzie suspicious. Besides, Mr. Poe didn't like to miss opportunities for treats from the meals.

I wondered what that necklace in the incident room could have told us. Or, perhaps, the necklace was part of the payday. We hadn't asked Nora if she was missing any jewelry. Well, maybe Kieran had. I would have to ask him later.

Or it could have belonged to Sarah. It had been hidden in that box with her passport. Maybe she'd planned to hock it and get out of Dodge.

Again, while I could make up scenarios as much as I wanted, Kieran would insist on proof.

One thing we knew was Sarah hadn't been the only one who knew about the diamond necklace. Someone had gone straight for the puzzle box and taken it.

After sneaking downstairs while everyone was at dinner, I looked through the guest book at the front desk and made quick notes of the room numbers. Then, using the map, I tried to figure out how to get to each room from behind the walls.

With my map in hand, I skipped the rooms where our neighbors on the court were staying. It turned out finding the secret entrances was easier behind the walls as there were easy to see levers.

The first room I checked was Maximillian's. Of course, it was by accident. I thought I was heading into Sally and Alex's room. My map was the opposite way round from what I'd thought.

He had several stacks of papers on his desk. After putting on my gloves, I carefully went through them.

The spreadsheets showed investments for the O'Sullivans. It appeared they were doing well, and I didn't understand why he was so worried about them.

His laptop was sitting on the desk. I opened it and was surprised to find it wasn't password protected. Some people weren't very bright when it came to protecting themselves from identity theft.

It didn't take me long to find the accounting program and to pull up the spreadsheets for the O'Sullivans. Numbers were my sister's thing, but the program was simple enough that I could figure it out.

I stared at them for a few minutes, before I realized that the numbers on the computer weren't as positive as the ones on the printouts. It looked like the O'Sullivans had taken some big hits financially. I compared the printouts to the computer. I was no forensic accountant, but things didn't match up. The question was, which set of records was the right one?

Was he stealing from them? If so, why would that lead him to kill the priest and the nun?

I took pictures with my phone of both sets of records. I was careful to put everything back the way I'd found it. Then I quietly went through his clothes and baggage searching for the necklace.

I didn't find anything.

I'd closed the secret passage door, and it took me a panicked minute to figure out that I had to push against the wall to open it again. Then it took two wrong turns and another twenty minutes to find the room that belonged to the Airendales.

Except for a few toiletries, nothing was left out in the room. Everything was so tidy it made me wonder if one of them might be OCD.

There were no electronics or papers. But when I pulled open one of the suitcases from the closet, I found several items that looked as though they'd been pilfered from around the castle. Nothing looked too expensive. Most of it was just trinkets.

After carefully putting everything back, I searched through some of the drawers in the wardrobe. I'm not sure what I hoped to find.

I was just about to slip out the secret passageway when a key jostled in the door. I dove under the bed because it was the closest place to hide.

Thank goodness the housekeepers here at the castle were great, as there wasn't a single dust bunny to be found.

"Why are you crying?" Alex asked, as they came into the room.

"Did you not notice?" Sally answered.

"Notice what?"

"How they were all staring at me? I'm certain they think I've done something." She sounded hysterical. And technically, she had stolen several items.

"Take a breath," he said. "I'm sure it's your imagination."

"Don't do that. I know what I saw and felt. Especially that couple from Shamrock Cove, Rob and Scott. They were watching me like hawks eyeing prey."

"I was right there beside you and didn't notice any of it."

"Because you were distracted by that beautiful supermodel sitting beside you."

He sighed. "She isn't a model. She's a photographer. We were talking cameras."

"Still, you didn't notice how those two men kept staring at me like I was a criminal."

"That is your guilty conscience," he said. "And you have been stealing. They may have seen you."

She sobbed. "You aren't helping."

"You're lucky the detective inspector hasn't arrested you," he said. "I thought the therapy was helping. I certainly spend enough on it."

"It was. At home, I could control it. But here there are so many shiny things... and it isn't like they will notice."

"Oh, no. We are not going home with all that stuff. Can you imagine what will happen if you are caught by customs trying to sneak those items into the U.S.? You have to claim it all. And if anything is reported stolen... you'll be in jail for a long time. And then what will your ladies who lunch crowd think?"

"You're just trying to scare me, and you know that doesn't work."

"I'm being honest with you. Maybe, a stint in jail is what you need."

She sobbed. "Why are you being like this?"

"Because I'm embarrassed, Sally, and I'm tired of covering up for you. I love you, but this has got to stop. Don't you realize this could ruin our business if you're found out? What will Nora and Gordon think? They're good people, who are trying so hard to do great things. How disappointed and angry do you think they would be if they knew what you'd done?"

She cried more, and then sat down on the bed.

I was embarrassed too, that I was privy to such an intimate

conversation. I also worried about how I'd be able to get out from under the bed.

"Go clean yourself up," he said. "They're playing games tonight and I want to go."

"I don't feel like it," she said.

"Too bad. I mean it. The very least you can do is go play a game with me. Besides, I'm not leaving you alone again. There is no way I can trust you."

His tone was mean, but it was more like he was disappointed. I couldn't imagine what the stress of living with someone who stole the way Sally did. I'm not sure I could have held my temper either.

They didn't speak for several minutes, but then water started running in the bathroom.

I took a deep breath when I heard the door click closed. Then I waited to make certain they had really left.

After nearly being caught, I decided to head back to my room. But, of course, I got turned around again. I was about to give up and just go through whatever room I found next when I finally found the right stairwell. I headed upstairs and turned to the left.

What I didn't see coming was the man, who grabbed me and put his hand over my mouth.

EIGHTEEN

"It's me," Kieran whispered in my ear. "I'm going to take my hand away, do not scream."

He let go, and I leaned down to pick up my phone where I'd dropped it on the stone. Thankfully, it was in a protective case, so it wasn't broken.

"You scared me to death," I whispered.

"Not here," he said. Then he half dragged me back to Lizzie and my room.

When the door creaked open, Lizzie and Mr. Poe were sitting on her bed with pensive looks on their faces. Well, I knew who'd told him to search for me.

I shook my head.

She wagged a finger at me. "Don't even," she said. "I've been waiting on you for half an hour. Rob and Scott are scouring the castle for you. When we couldn't find you, I texted Kieran. I was worried the killer had you."

I sighed. "I'm fine," I said.

"Well, I didn't know that, did I? You couldn't be bothered to tell me you were going snooping." She picked up Mr. Poe and hugged him. "Or at the very least, leave me a note. I thought you might be dead." She sniffed, and it was obvious how upset she was.

"I'm sorry," I said. "I never meant to worry you. But I knew you'd try to stop me if I told you what I'd planned."

"With good reason," Kieran interjected. "We're dealing with a killer who has murdered two people. It isn't safe for you to go traipsing off alone. I believe we've had this conversation before. You can't scare us like that."

It was obvious he was worried about me. That moment when he held me close flashed through my brain, and my cheeks heated.

"Fine. I'm sorry that I worried you both. I thought since dinner was going on that I could use that time to do a bit of searching. Do you want to know what I've found out or not?"

His eyebrows went up.

Lizzie rolled her eyes. "First, promise me you won't do something dumb like that again."

I made the cross-my-heart sign that we used to do as kids. For us, it was sacred. "Promise."

"Okay. Now, tell us what you found," she said.

Kieran flipped open his notebook.

"I'll text you the pictures I took in the accountant's room. I don't know much about spreadsheets, but I do understand enough that I could see he had two sets of books for the O'Sullivans. What was on his computer is different than the printouts. Like, maybe they aren't having the money troubles they think they are."

"And maybe he's embezzling?" Lizzie asked, as she looked over my shoulder. She was great with numbers. She pointed to the printout. "That's what it looks like to me. He's skimming, a lot from what I can see." Then she pointed to a row of numbers on the computer. "Like at least a hundred thousand off this account alone.

"I knew there was something about that guy," she said. "He

has beady eyes, and he's always glancing around like someone is trying to attack him at any moment."

"He feels guilty," Kieran said. "When I was interviewing him, he kept saying he wanted his lawyer. I had to convince him it wasn't that kind of chat we were having. But you've gained access illegally to this proof," he said. "There is no way I can use it."

"Yes, but you're trying to find a killer. What's adding one more room to your request for a warrant?" I said. "You were going to do that anyway. And if you happened upon this information that you know is there—you could save the O'Sullivans a lot of grief."

"You make it all sound so easy."

"Isn't it, though? You play golf with the judge, and you went to school together. I'm betting since it is pouring down raining, that he's no longer fishing. I'm sure you can get your warrants soon."

"How do you know I went to school with him?"

I laughed. "Your very proud grandmother, plus I spend a lot of time in the bookstore. It's as big a gossip hub as the Crown and Clover pub is some days."

He chuckled but it wasn't a happy sound. "Nothing is sacred in Shamrock Cove," he mumbled. "Sometimes I miss the anonymity of working in a bigger city."

"Well, you should get a warrant for everyone's rooms, and that way no one can say anything," I said. "There is also a suitcase full of stolen items in the Airendales' room.

"Oh, and while you're at it, get one for the staff quarters as well. We should go over everything and recheck things."

"What's happening in there?" He pointed toward my head.

"Well, we said it before, but it's making sense. Before the guests arrived, there was someone here who had found out about the treasure, whatever it is the priest and nun came looking for in the castle. If you ask me, it's a priceless piece of art. Otherwise, why would they have been looking through those logs?"

"We've been through them over and over," Kieran said. "What we see there doesn't add up with what has been covered by insurance."

"Which makes Maximillian look more guilty of a financial crime, but why would he kill the priest and nun? Is it possible whoever is doing this knows about the accountant's duplicity? I mean, if there is a real treasure, or if the artwork is worth more than everyone thinks, then that could be motive to kill as well. Like maybe they were working with the accountant or another insider."

"What about the diamond necklace?" he asked.

"The theft of that piece of jewelry ties the killer to Sarah at least. Sometimes diamonds have codes imbedded into them so if they are stolen they can be returned to the rightful owners. If it was stolen, it might lead us to the thief. But that is just one small part of this.

"You need to make the O'Sullivans give us access to wherever they store the things that aren't out in the castle. Every house has a storeroom or an attic. Or they may use an outbuilding. Perhaps whatever it is the killer is looking for may be in there."

"Us?"

"Yes. Please, Kieran. The storm will be over in the morning, and you're going to lose all your suspects. We need those warrants, and I need to see the storage room."

"We'll see," he said. "Is that all you discovered during your snooping?"

I grimaced.

"What did you do?"

"I was sort of accidentally in the Airendales room when they came back in," I said.

My sister gasped. "Did they catch you?"

I cleared my throat. "No. I hid under the bed."

Lizzie laughed out loud. Even Kieran smiled.

"You're lucky they didn't see you," he said.

"I know. I wasn't super proud of myself. But I overheard them arguing about her little problem. I think he was giving her some tough love. He was very unhappy with her. But they didn't say a word about the murders. Everything was focused on her kleptomania. She was in tears, and he was fed up. He said he was tired of paying for her therapy, and that she never gets better."

Kieran spoke over his SAT phone to Sheila. "I need warrants."

"Already done, boss. We have them for the castle and the grounds. I called when the internet was working earlier."

"She's always thinking ahead."

"She is a wonder." I said. "It's a big place," I said. "I don't suppose you need some help?"

He snorted. "Better to keep you by my side rather than let you run around alone."

"I like the way you think," I joked.

He shook his head.

"Where do we search first?"

"Well, thanks to you we know that the Airendales and the accountant have something to hide. Maybe they killed to protect themselves if the victims were on to them. I'll have the team search those rooms first. We'll focus on whatever storage the O'Sullivans have."

There was a loud boom of thunder. Lizzie and I jumped, and Mr. Poe barked.

Kieran didn't even flinch.

"I thought when we moved away from Texas, we wouldn't have to deal with thunderstorms anymore," Lizzie said. "It's just as loud and even wilder here so close to the sea."

"It can be," Kieran said. "But there's nothing to worry about.

We are in for some flooding and winds, but you're safe." He was always so gentle with my sister. I appreciated him for that, even though he saved all of his cynicism and snark for me.

It was okay, I could take it. In that way, we spoke the same language. The psychiatrist my detective sometimes consulted in my books would have all kinds of things to say about that.

In real life, I tried not to analyze our relationship. My sister believed he had feelings for me. I wasn't so sure. If I thought too hard about it, it became confusing. We liked spending time together and when he touched me... well, I liked it.

"Well, you're not leaving me here," Lizzie said. "I'm coming with you."

"It might be better if you attend the games they are playing. You can keep an eye on the players and text us if anything goes hinky," I said.

"So, I'd be undercover?"

"Yes," I said, knowing that would appeal to her. As much as she complained about my snooping, she couldn't resist solving a mystery.

"Fine. But you have to promise to be careful."

"I will. And we'll walk you down so you won't be alone."

A half-hour later, the search began. The guests were all involved in the games. The wording in Kieran's warrant meant he did not have to announce the search. For now, he felt like it might be best if the guests were unaware. His team split into three and went searching for the evidence I'd already found, and anything else they came across.

Kieran and I headed downstairs to one of the many storage areas the O'Sullivans had. Nora had made Kieran a map. It was much colder and damper down there. I was wishing I'd brought a much warmer sweater.

With the master key Gordon gave Kieran, he was able to

open the heavy wooden door. The O'Sullivans were the only ones who knew we were doing a search. Kieran hadn't told them that Sally and their accountant had both been stealing from them. They thought this was about the deaths of the priest and nun.

He found a round switch on the wall and turned on the lights. The storeroom area went on for as far as the eye could see.

The bad part was there were so many things lying all over the place. Beautiful paintings were stacked against the walls. Unlit chandeliers hung from the ceiling. And there were long wooden tables holding a variety of vases, crystal, statues, and other items.

"There is no way we can go through all of this," I said. "It's so much more than I imagined."

"Well, I have a list of the current inventory that is supposed to be here. It goes from the most expensive item to the least."

"Where did you get that?"

"Mrs. O'Sullivan compiled it for me. When I asked her about the logs in the study, she said they'd moved everything online years ago. Supposedly, everything has been appraised."

"Then why were the criminals looking through the logs?"

"Could be they weren't aware that this existed."

"From the dust and the lack of footprints, I'd say we're the first people in here for some time. I mean, it's a temperature-controlled room, I'm sure to keep the art from fading. But keeping dust out in an old castle like this must be difficult."

He glanced around the room. "I thought we'd check the pricier items to make certain they're still here."

"Okay, Detective Inspector, where do we begin?"

"A Caravaggio," he said.

"Wow. That's quite the piece," I said, glancing at the picture on the paper. "I wonder where it is."

"This says it is valued at seventy-five thousand," he said.

"Uh. Are you sure you read that right? More like seventy-five million. And it's sitting down here where no one can see it. It's kind of sad."

"Look." He showed me the paper. It was listed for seventy-five thousand. I was no expert but I knew enough about art to understand that was woefully underpriced.

"Why would they be so unaware of how much their painting is worth?"

"Because someone told them they are fakes. The accountant must have been working with the appraiser to devalue their collection. Then I bet he planned to sneak down here and steal things one by one."

"But he would have to show provenance," Kieran said.

"True, but I think things are more fluid on the black market."

"So the scheme is to dupe the O'Sullivans into thinking their collection is worth nothing. Meanwhile, he would be selling things on the black market."

"Yes. And the priest and nun, who weren't either of those things, found out about it. Maybe they wanted a piece of the action and he bumped them off. Or we have a fourth suspect somewhere."

"You may be on to something there. But wouldn't they know from the records that their items were real?"

It was a good question. "Not if some expert hired by Maximillian came in and told them otherwise."

"If you're right, they may be sitting on a gold mine."

"Exactly."

"I can't even comprehend that kind of wealth. That's more your league," he said.

I laughed hard. "Kieran, I may move in certain circles, but I'm not friends with people like that. I know some, yes. But my friends are down to earth, and most of them are writers. They are usually the only people who understand how my mind works."

"And how is that?"

"You've met me. I am extremely nosy, and I talk to myself."

"Two things we have in common," he said.

"The nosy thing is your job," I said. "But I had no idea you talked to yourself." I didn't think I'd ever seen him do that.

"Usually, I'm at home or in my office. Sheila's caught me a few times. It's how I work things out."

"Same, but with me there are a bunch of characters that I'm having conversations with too."

He laughed. "Well, I'm grateful I don't have that. I don't know how you do it."

"There are lots of memes about how some people get a straitjacket, others are called writers."

We both chuckled.

"This is going to take forever," I said as I peeked under another covered painting to see if it was the Caravaggio. At the same time, I kept a running tab of the artists I'd seen so far, including a Turner. While I was no art expert, I'd studied the subject extensively. The brush strokes on the Turner were distinctive. These paintings absolutely looked real. At the very least, they needed a second and third opinion.

"Let me see that sheet, please," I said.

He handed it to me. The light wasn't great down here, so I used the app on my phone.

"I wonder who put this list together and the last time they had appraisals done. These are not correct."

"What do you mean?"

"These are undervalued by millions."

He'd been looking under one of the sheets hanging over another painting.

"Are you sure?"

"Well, like I said, I'm no expert, but I had to do research when I had an art thief in one of my books. If these paintings are real, and I have no reason to think they aren't, we're talking about the appraisals being off by millions.

"You said that Nora put this report together."

"She printed it off." He flipped through it. "But it was provided by the accountant."

"The initials on the spreadsheet are M.H. Maximillian Herbert," I said. "Not only is he stealing money from them, he undervalued their collection. I bet they have no idea what they are sitting on here."

"But why would they believe him?"

"I think I have an idea." I pulled the cover up on another painting. It was by a Dutch artist that I recognized.

"He tells them their stuff isn't worth much, so they leave it in storage. He has supposed experts who are working with him, probably for a cut of the proceeds. Then he sneaks around and steals it, selling it at an enormous profit."

"But like I said before, wouldn't whoever bought it need the provenance?"

I shrugged. "That's probably what the priest was searching for in the study. But there are all kinds of ways to fake that sort of thing, especially on the black market. This is the treasure the journals refer to and the poor O'Sullivans have absolutely been duped."

"Do you think Maximillian's the killer?"

I blew out a breath. "I mean, we've had cases where we've underestimated killers before. And we know he's cheating the O'Sullivans by cooking their books and undervaluing their collection. Is it such a stretch to believe he could be a killer?"

"There are no connections between him and the victims, though. I couldn't find a single trail that led back to Sarah and Carl."

"I have to admit that I just can't see him as a killer. Maybe he was an accomplice. The way he's cheating the poor O'Sullivans makes him a bit smarter than I'd given him credit for. I can't believe they haven't discovered him stealing their money."

"He's related to the family," Kieran said. "That came up in our search. He is a distant cousin. That may be why they've kept him on. That and they can't possibly know what he's been doing."

"He probably feels like he's owed an inheritance. Men like him always have some sort of justification. His father worked for them, as well. We know that, and it is possible that Carl and Sarah were his accomplices."

"Question is: did he kill off his partners?"

I was about to answer when the lights flickered out, and a door slammed.

"What was that?"

Kieran used his flashlight to find the path back to the door. When we got there, it was shut. He tried the handle.

"It's locked," he said.

"Who would do that? At least, you have the key."

"Except it locks from the outside. There's no keyhole on this side of the door."

I tried turning the knob that controlled the lights. Nothing happened.

Great.

We were locked in a dark room with no way out.

NINETEEN

I took a deep breath. At least the storage room was huge. I had a thing about small dark spaces. It helped that Kieran was there, too. He was always so calm and collected.

"I'll just try to text my sister," I said. But the text went nowhere. "The signal is out again. Do you have any bars?"

He sighed. "No. It probably went out with the power. And I left my SAT phone in the evidence room when your sister was worried about you earlier and came to make me search for you."

"But when your people realize they can't get in touch with you they will figure out where we are, right?"

"Except that I didn't tell them."

Great. "Well, we told Nora we were looking into things, and when my sister can't find me, she will search the place. And I think I mentioned we were coming down here. It's just a matter of when she realizes we aren't around. I suggest we stay busy until she figures it out. Otherwise, my anxiety might kick in."

I'm a strong woman, but the idea my sister might not find me caused my insides to twist. I forced myself to breathe again.

Kieran took my hand in his and squeezed. His touch had a calming effect, and the warmth of him seeped through me.

"How do you suggest we do that in the dark?" He didn't sound annoyed, more inquisitive.

"I have at least a ten-hour charge on my phone, and I carry a charger bank in my pocket." I prayed we weren't down here long enough to find out how long my phone would last. "While we're searching through the paintings, we can talk about who might have locked us in," I said. "Someone isn't happy with us being down here."

"Top of that suspect list would be the accountant."

I nodded, even though he couldn't see me. "Agreed. But is he working alone? When we left, he was in the room with the others, playing the mystery game."

"It doesn't mean he couldn't sneak down here and lock the door."

"True. Maybe the killings weren't pre-meditated. The killer perhaps tried to reason with Sarah, but when she wouldn't listen, he or she strangled and drowned her. Same with Carl. Maybe, they were asking for a bigger cut of the profits."

"It has to be someone strong to strangle her," he said. "And the water wasn't that deep, so someone powerful held her down."

"Okay, stay with me," I said. "If the killer was Maximillian, would he have the strength? He's tall, pasty, and quite thin. I just don't see him doing either killing."

"People can surprise you."

"True. And I know you need evidence and not gut instincts, but I really don't see him as a killer. I keep saying that, but it's true. Though, it's obvious he's ripping off his clients in a big way."

"Like you said before, he could be working with someone who works on-site. That's what the evidence is telling us," he said. "Well, you're correct about one thing."

"What's that?" I asked.

"I can't go by your gut instincts. I need evidence."

I sighed.

"We keep going in circles," I said. "At least, we've caught one criminal, even if it isn't for the murders. And you can stop Maximillian. The O'Sullivans are going to be so shocked to discover they are millionaires several times over. I can't believe what he's been doing to them.

"And what will happen when you arrest Sally?"

"That will depend on the O'Sullivans and if they want to press charges, since it's obvious she has a psychological problem. You heard them talking about her therapy, and the court will look kindly on the fact that she's been trying to get help. She may just get probation. Again, depends on the O'Sullivans."

"I wonder if your team have found the evidence of the theft, and Maximilian's fraud."

"I'm sure they have."

"Do you think the lights going out really have to do with the storm?"

"Are you asking whether someone is planning something tonight? It's possible."

"I'm worried about Lizzie. She may be in a room with a killer, and we are stuck down here. Someone wanted us trapped."

Panic rose tight in my chest.

"We need to get out of here," I said. "What if she's in danger?"

"How do you propose we do that? The lock is on the other side of the door."

"Right, but the secret passages run along every floor. Why should this one be any different? Let's look for another entrance."

It took nearly an hour of us moving things away from the wall and searching for something that looked like a lever or feeling for air coming through the wall. We were at the far end of the room when we finally had some luck.

"There is air coming through the mortar here," I said. I pushed on the wall but nothing happened. "Do you see any kind of handle or lever?"

"No." He ran his hands across the back wall.

"It has to be here." I tried pushing harder on the stones, and there was a slight give. "I think it's stuck. Come help me."

He moved beside me, his pine-scented cologne filling my senses. I wasn't sure how he always smelled like a fresh forest, but he did.

This isn't the time to think about that sort of thing. But his scent had a calming effect on my nerves.

"It feels like it hasn't been opened in some time," he said. "With all the dust, probably no one has been here in months or maybe even years."

"Which makes me wonder why, if they were planning to steal something, our killer hadn't been down here."

"If they were in league with the accountant maybe they didn't need to yet."

"Or they were looking for another way in. We kept hearing someone inside the walls. Maybe they've been trying to find a secret entrance to the storage room all this time. Gordon said he never let the key out of his sight when he gave it to you.

"They could have been trying to find a way to take things out of this room without anyone seeing them."

"That is true," he said. "Let's give it a hard shoulder. On three."

He counted down, and we hit the wall hard. It shifted slightly. Not enough to get through, but at least we'd found what we'd been looking for. After four tries, it was open enough for us to slip through.

From the cobwebs covering the walls, it appeared no one had been down here in years. I would need a shower and good scrub from head to toe. I didn't mind spiders when they were outside, but I had a completely different opinion when I had to walk through their webs.

I shivered.

"I'll go first," Kieran said as if he could read my mind. "There should be a stairway at the end of the passageway."

I hoped he was right.

Even with the light from his phone, it was so dark. It took us a few minutes to find the stairs. And climbing them was slow, as we tried to figure out where we were.

"Let's try that door," I said when we'd gone up a flight of stairs. "Maybe we will be in the main part of the house and can figure out our next move."

He nodded.

As he pushed open the door there was a chilling scream and then a crash.

I recognized that scream. I'd heard it before.

Lizzie was in trouble.

TWENTY

I took off at a run toward the scream with Kieran close on my heels. I had to find my sister.

"Who was that?" he asked. "Do you know?"

"It's Lizzie."

"Be careful," he said. "Do you even know where we are?"

I shone my flashlight around. "Near the kitchen," I said. "We have to find her." I ran toward the kitchen, barely avoiding colliding with the huge built-in cabinet outside the door leading into it.

"Stop," he said. "Let me get my walkie-talkie from the incident room so I can call the team for help. Stay here. I'll be right back."

He left, but I kept moving forward.

"Lizzie? Where are you?"

I was met by an eerie silence. My stomach rumbled with nerves and adrenaline soared through my veins. Mr. Poe barked ferociously. She was in trouble.

The mudroom door to the outside was open, and rain pelted through onto the stone floor. I grabbed one of the jackets by the door and pulled the hood up over my head. Then I slipped my feet into some wellies that were a good size too big. I didn't care.

The wind was crazy, and I could barely walk against it. The rain pelted down so hard that it hurt through the jacket and my jeans. This wasn't the normally soft rain we'd grown used to in Shamrock Cove.

When I reached the pond, a black blur became visible. Mr. Poe ran toward me, barking his head off. He seldom barked unless something was wrong.

"Where is she?"

He was running with his leash attached but my sister was very much missing. I picked up the muddy leash and he pulled me forward.

For several minutes we fought the weather, and I was beginning to wonder if our dog had any idea where he was going.

"We need to find Lizzie," I said, in case he'd misunderstood our mission.

He barked and continued to pull me forward. What had she been doing out here and why had she screamed?

I didn't want to think the worst, but the truth was inevitable. Someone had her.

Dread curdled my stomach. We had to find her.

He pulled me toward a glass building that looked like a nursery. At the entrance, Mr. Poe barked again. It took all my strength to open the glass door against the wind, but I did it. The place was pitch-black, though.

At least the rain wasn't slicing through my skin.

"Lizzie, are you in here?"

Nothing, except for the rain pounding on the glass and the howl of the wind.

But Mr. Poe kept pulling on the leash. There was a rake by the door, and I grabbed it. I had no idea what was going on, but I might need a weapon.

Our dog slunk forward, growling menacingly. If I let go of

the leash, I had a feeling he would attack whoever was in the darkness. I was not about to let him get hurt.

We'd gone about halfway through the building when he stopped, and his growl became a worried bark.

"If you take one more step, I'll kill her," a deep, gravelly voice said in the darkness. I couldn't see anyone. I reached for my phone, but it must have fallen out of my pocket as I ran.

"I'm not moving," I said.

Mr. Poe barked, and I shushed him.

"Mercy, don't let him hurt you or Mr. Poe," my sister begged. "Just do what he wants."

"Please, don't hurt her," I said. "I'll do whatever you want."

"If you hadn't been snooping, none of this would be necessary," the man growled. It took me a minute, but I recognized his voice. It was Jim, the gardener. He'd seemed like such a kind and knowledgeable man.

I cleared my throat. "The police already know it was the accountant who murdered the priest and the nun. I'm not sure why you've taken my sister," I lied. "We're good at keeping secrets. If you want the treasure for yourself, you can just let her go, and we won't say a word."

"I'm not stupid," he said.

"Of course you aren't." Why hadn't I listened to Kieran and stayed put? I could have really used his help.

"Okay. Are you saying you killed them? Did they do something terrible? You seem like a nice man. I'm sure you have your reasons for doing what you did."

"Why would I tell you anything?"

"You make a good point, but there just might be a possibility that I can help you find a way out of this, and you don't have to hurt my sister or me. I just need to know why. Were you working with Maximillian and the others and they tried to cheat you?"

"You have it all wrong."

I sighed. At least, as long as I kept him talking, he wasn't hurting us. I didn't care so much about myself, but I had to save Lizzie.

"Okay. So not Maximillian. But the priest and the nun."

"Blasphemous, those two pretending to be what they weren't. Saw my picture in an article about the castle, didn't they? Then they threatened to expose me to the O'Sullivans if I didn't work with them. And they wanted to steal from them. The O'Sullivans have been kind and given me a chance to change my life for the better. I wasn't about to let those two ruin my life again."

"So, you worked with them before?" I tried to see if I could find another weapon, but there was very little light. I was on my own against a man who outweighed me by a good fifty pounds and was several inches taller than me too.

I had Krav Maga training, but I was worried my sister might be injured if I went on the attack. I needed a plan.

"Years ago. I had a different name, and I was a different person. I tried to change my life. I was going straight, and then they came and ruined everything."

"I can see how you might have been frustrated. What did they want you to do?"

"Carl read some story about a treasure being hidden in the castle. He wanted to find it. I tried to explain none of it was true. It would have been found long ago. But he wouldn't let up. Came up with a scheme, didn't he?

"Then she showed up." I assumed he was talking about the would-be nun. "Carl wasn't happy with her being here as she was supposed to come later when he'd tracked down the treasure. They threatened me, said if I didn't help them search for the storage room, they'd out me.

"It's not my fault they are dead. The pair of them left me no choice. I had to protect the O'Sullivans. They have given me purpose and a new life. I wouldn't do anything to hurt them."

"But you did hurt them. You smashed a whiskey bottle on Gordon's head."

"I didn't mean to hurt him. My nerves were in tatters and he surprised me in the distillery and I lashed out without thinking. Then I couldn't summon help as I shouldn't have been in there and didn't want to draw any suspicion my way."

"That makes sense," I said softly. "You killed Carl and Sarah because they were ruining everything for you. But why then did you steal the diamond necklace from Sarah's puzzle box in the incident room?"

"I knew she had kept that trinket in the box from the last job we did together. Enough time has passed now that I could sell it and make myself a little money at the same time. Something for all my trouble. I just want to be left alone to tend to my gardens."

"I understand. But my sister and I had nothing to do with any of this. Please, let us go."

"Can't do that now, can I? You know the truth. Have to do you both in. I don't want to. I take no pleasure in hurting women and you seem like good people. But I'm not giving up my life here for anyone. I need my gardens."

"Then that's two more murders added to your count, and why? I bet with the others, since they were criminals, you could plead self-defense. I write a lot of mysteries, and I've seen that happen before."

I was grasping, but it wasn't my life I was trying to save. I had to do whatever it took to protect Lizzie and Mr. Poe. I glanced down at him. He was still pulling on the leash, trying to get to Lizzie, but it was as if he understood the danger.

My heartbeat double-timed in my chest, and I could barely breathe because of the nerves.

The gardener didn't say anything. Maybe, he was thinking about my crazy plan.

Then an arm snaked around my neck, and he pulled me

tight against him. Had he been behind me the whole time? So much for my detective skills. And where was my sister?

"Run, Lizzie," I screamed hoarsely as the arm tightened around my neck.

What is he, some kind of ninja?

I hadn't heard or seen him move in the dark.

He squeezed my neck so hard that there were black spots in my eyes. But I couldn't give in. If he killed me, Lizzie would be next.

I let go of Mr. Poe's leash, and he darted off.

My training kicked in. Using all of my strength, I twisted in his arms and shoved the fist that wasn't holding the rake into his throat.

He grunted and stumbled back, and I followed, swinging the rake with all my might. It hit him hard and the tines scraped his face. As he reached up, I kicked at his knees, first one and then the other. He fell.

I roundhouse-kicked at his head, and then swung the rake again. Just as he hit the ground flat, a light blinded me.

"It's me," Kieran called out. "You're under arrest," he said to the lump on the ground.

As much as I wanted to fall to my knees, as I'd just used every bit of energy, I had to find my sister.

"Lizzie, where are you?" I cried out.

There was no answer.

I stumbled forward, trying to find her. Kieran's flashlight lit the way to a limp form on the ground just in front of me.

"Please God, let her be okay," I whispered as I ran toward her.

She was unconscious, but she had a pulse. Mr. Poe sat next to her like a statue. He was protecting her.

"Kieran, help."

Several people entered the greenhouse at once.

"We've got her, miss," one of Kieran's men said.

"She's unconscious but she has a pulse," I said. "Please, help her."

"We are," one of them said kindly.

At the same time, two more men arrived to escort Jim out of the greenhouse. I was surprised he could walk. I had hoped I'd broken his knees.

Maybe it was mean, but I was happy to see he had a limp at least.

I heard something snap, and then my sister's eyes blinked open. She started to fight the men.

"It's okay," I said. "They're here to help."

"Are you okay?" she asked. "I knew you'd find me."

"That she did," Kieran said from behind me. "And nearly killed the suspect. He's lucky we showed up when we did. You're going to have to show me some of those Krav Maga moves you used."

He said the last part as a joke, and I was glad. I'd been on the verge of tears, more so because I was grateful my sister was okay.

Still, my knees nearly gave out, and Kieran was there, putting his arm around my shoulders. "You'll be okay," he said. "You've just had a bit of a shock."

"Thanks for not yelling at me."

He chuckled. "Oh, you're not getting off that easy. I will be yelling later. But only after we get you warm and into some dry clothes. Come on, let's get you both back to the house so we can assess your injuries."

"I'm fine," I said.

"We'll see about that." Kieran kept his arm around me as we trudged through the rain and mud to the house.

I was freezing by the time we made it back. He wrapped me in a warm blanket that Nora gave him. I shivered even though I was enveloped in warmth.

Shock was weird that way.

"Where is Lizzie?" Rob asked. Our crew were all in the kitchen.

"My team is bringing her in," Kieran said. "She was injured."

"So was Mercy," Brenna said. "Look at her neck."

I waved away their concern. "I'm really okay."

"They're right," Kieran said. "You are injured. Why didn't you say something?" He reached for me, and gently touched my neck. A new warmth spread through my body that had nothing to do with the blanket.

"Get some ice," Lolly said. "You're going to have some bruising, but maybe we can stop the swelling."

They all fussed over me and my sister for several hours. We were so lucky to have such lovely friends. Rob and Scott gave Mr. Poe a bath in their room. After a hot shower, I almost felt back to normal.

I dressed in my warmest PJs. When I came out of the bathroom, our friends were all waiting for me in the bedroom. Kieran was in the corner with his notebook open.

"Tell us everything," Scott said.

And so, I did.

TWENTY-ONE

A day later, we were back at Number Three. I'd never been so grateful for our house and a regular routine. Lizzie was feeling better but still staying at home. She'd taken quite the hit to the head. She was fine, but I made her take a few days away from the bookstore. Her assistant Caro had things well in hand.

Lizzie was in the kitchen baking, which was her idea of relaxation, and I had just sat down at my desk when the doorbell rang.

"I'll get it," I said.

After glancing through the small window in the door, I frowned. It was Lolly and Kieran.

What are they doing here?

We'd given our statements the day before. And like always when we were involved in an investigation, Kieran had let us listen to Jim make his case. Turned out he'd borrowed that name from a dead guy.

To protect the O'Sullivans from any blowback, he told the police everything. How he'd been a part of Carl and Sarah's original gang. How she'd turned on them, and then thought she could pick up where they'd left off when they had finished their prison sentences. His real name was John Brady, and he had an incredibly long rap-sheet.

Carl and Sarah were working against the O'Sullivans, who he now saw as family. In his mind, he was protecting them from outside forces. In his way, he had done whatever it took to save his new family.

As for Sally, the O'Sullivans had refused to post charges against her.

Their accountant cousin was not so lucky. He would be doing some prison time. I'd learned that from Lolly. She said the O'Sullivans were bringing in a forensic accountant and new appraisers, both recommended by law enforcement.

"Morning," I said as I opened the door. "What's this all about?"

"I came to check on your sister," Lolly said. "Kieran said he had some details from the case to discuss with you."

"Oh?" I glanced over Lolly's shoulder at him. "I thought we were finished with all that."

"I have a few follow-up questions," he said.

"Is that what the kids call it these days?" Lolly asked.

She pushed past me, laughing as she went down the hall.

"What was that about?" I said, blushing slightly.

He shrugged. "I never know with her."

"Well, come in. Do you want a cup of coffee?"

"Actually..." He held up two cups. "I brought you one from the pub."

I smiled. We were both caffeine addicts. "That's kind of you. Since your gran is in the kitchen, why don't we go into my office?"

He nodded and followed me down the hallway and to the left. I loved my office. It had an old-school Agatha Christie feel with the period furniture to match. This had once been our grandfather's home, and he had excellent taste. We hadn't had to update anything.

"So, what's going on?" I asked as we sat in the chairs in front of my desk. "Did something new happen in the case?"

"We were able to tie the gardener's DNA to what we'd found on the priest's robes. So we have evidence to back up the confession. You and your sister probably won't have to testify since we have a confession."

I took a deep breath. "That's a relief. I wasn't worried about me, but I'm not sure how Lizzie might have taken all that." She was the more sensitive twin, and I didn't think her nerves would handle a court case very well.

"Why were there no bloody footprints left at the scene?" I asked. It had been bothering me.

"They'd been standing outside on the patio, through the French doors behind the desk. So, the blood was washed away in the rain, and the priest stumbled back into the chair."

"Did the gardener stick with his story about trying to protect the O'Sullivans?"

"He did. I'm inclined to believe him. After several hours of questioning, it was clear he'd grown protective of them because they had given him a second chance. He also used the passage-ways to keep an eye on things inside the estate."

I blinked. "Wow. How do they feel about that?"

"They are in shock on all counts. As you might imagine, they had no idea of the worth of their possessions. They are already working with a new appraiser. But they've decided to continue with their bookings and tours."

"I'm not sure if I was sitting on that kind of money, I'd want to go to so much trouble."

He laughed. "Aren't you, though?"

I shook my head. "I do well, but not billionaire well. Besides, I'm perfectly happy here in Number Three with my sister."

He chuckled.

"What?"

"That's one of the things I like about you. That you like a simple life. Well, that is when you aren't trying to get yourself killed solving a murder."

He made a fair point.

Then he sighed and frowned.

"What is it?"

"Well, I didn't want to trouble you so soon after what happened, but I need your help."

"Is it with a case?"

He stood and shut the door to my office.

This must be serious.

"Of sorts. One of my men was going through some footage looking for a shoplifter."

"At Lizzie's store?"

"No. It was at another establishment. The thing is, we noticed something else."

"I'm intrigued."

"Do you remember being in Kelly's two weeks ago?"

"Yes, I was buying new wellies. With the weather here, I realized that I needed two pairs so one lot could dry out while I wore the others."

"Right." He pulled some photos out of his pocket.

"Do you remember seeing this man in the store?"

He pointed to a gray-haired man. I couldn't really see his face.

"No. I don't think so. I was busy writing my book in my head when I was there. I really wasn't paying attention to my surroundings."

His eyebrows lifted.

"I know. I know. But I'm on a deadline. I can't always control when the characters want to have conversations in my head. Why? Did he steal something?"

"No. How about here? This gives you a better look at his face." The man was standing just outside our bookstore and peering into the window. He'd glanced up at one of the CCTV cameras.

There was something about his eyes that seemed familiar.

"Who is he?"

"We don't know," he said. "He's now a John Doe at the hospital. He was hit by car a few days ago. The thing is, he isn't able, or is refusing, to tell us who he is. But we have a lot of CCTV footage of him watching you and your sister."

I shivered. "Do you think he's my stalker from New York?" That was the first thing that flashed through my brain.

"He has an Irish accent. It could all be a coincidence, but I find it strange that he's clearly been watching you and your sister."

"Yeah, that's not creepy at all."

"It's a lot to ask, but I wondered if you might come with me to the hospital."

"You want me to confront a stalker?"

One of the reasons I'd left New York was because I no longer felt safe there. Someone kept entering my apartment and moving things around. And every time I went walking around the city, it felt like someone was watching me.

After I'd returned to Texas to bury our mother, and then Lizzie's fiancé and his daughter, I had no desire to go back to Manhattan. And I thought we'd be safe here in Ireland, but we'd both felt like someone had been watching us since we'd arrived.

"We can make it so it isn't face-to-face, if you prefer."

"You've met me," I said.

"Yes. Which was why I thought you might want to confront him yourself."

He was right. If this was the man who had caused me so much trouble, I had more than a few words for him.

"Just me, though. I don't want my sister involved. At least, let me see if I can figure out if he's dangerous or not. When?"

"Do you have time now?"

My curiosity was at an all-time high. "Yes. Let me tell Lizzie I'm helping you with something. Give me a few minutes."

When we arrived at the hospital, Kieran stopped in front of a door.

"Before we go in, how did he end up here?" I asked him.

"Sheila found him on the side of the road when she was coming back from Dublin. He'd been hit by a car. Broke his arm. She said he was out of sorts, as in he couldn't remember who he was."

"Like amnesia? That is highly unlikely."

"So, you're a doctor now?" He smiled when he said it.

"No. But I did a lot of research for one of my books. Amnesia isn't very common."

"He took a pretty big whack to the head. And she said it was more as if he was confused. Are you ready?"

I nodded. "Best to just rip the Band-Aid off."

He pushed open the door. The room was empty. Kieran backed out and checked the room number again.

Then he frowned.

"What is it?" I asked.

"He should be in there. I don't know where he could have gone."

I followed Kieran down to the nurses' station.

"What happened to the gentleman in 103?" he asked.

The nurse shook her head. "He disappeared sometime in the night. Didn't bother to check himself out. He just vanished."

Kieran frowned.

"That's weird, right?" I said, nervously.

"Maybe," he said. "If he was up to no good, he may not have

wanted to stick around. I'll circulate his picture. We'll find him."

"Do you think we need to worry?"

Kieran shook his head. "No. If he wanted to confront you, he most likely already would have. He could just be a fan who is curious about you."

For most authors that might help the ego, but I was annoyed. "Maybe so. I still think my sister and I should be careful."

"That's always a good idea."

When I arrived home, Lizzie called for me from the kitchen. "Late lunch is ready," she said. Mr. Poe barked. I headed to the back of the house. The kitchen smelled of cottage pie, which was one of my favorites.

"I want to eat the air," I said.

She smiled. "It's one of the recipes Nora gave me. Where did Kieran take you?"

I wanted to protect her, and I didn't want her to worry about a possible stalker.

"He wanted to see if I could identify someone at the hospital, but the patient had already checked out."

She turned and then cocked her head. "Why would you know who it was?"

"He was a John Doe," I said truthfully. "Kieran will be circulating his picture around town. He seemed confused when they brought him in. As in, he didn't know his name."

"Poor man," she said compassionately. That was my sister.

"Yeah, just keep an eye out," I said. I showed her the picture that Kieran had texted me.

"Hmmm. I think I've seen him around the bookstore, but we've been so busy, I could be mistaking him for someone else. I'll keep an eye out, though.

"Oh, I have something funny to tell you."

"What's that?"

"I went out to the garden with Mr. Poe a little while ago. He sat in front of the fairy garden and grunted several times, like he was trying to talk to the flowers there. Or," she said laughing, "it could have been the fairies."

I laughed with her. "He's a very smart dog, maybe he speaks fairy. Do you, Mr. Poe?"

He cocked his head and yapped.

We giggled.

I loved our little family, and our friends. Shamrock Cove was home and always would be.

But the idea that some strange man had been watching us—well, I'd be keeping a close eye on my sister. I'd never allow anyone to hurt her or Mr. Poe. Maybe it was time for me to do a bit of investigating into this strange man.

"Mercy?"

I lifted my head. "What?"

"Are you sure nothing is wrong? You have a weird look on your face."

"Everything is fine." And it would be. We had an idyllic life in Shamrock Cove and I would never allow a stranger to ruin it.

A LETTER FROM LUCY CONNELLY

Dear reader,

Thank you for reading *Death at Inishmore Castle*. I'm grateful to you and I hope you enjoyed this latest installment of the Mercy and Lizzie mysteries. If you enjoyed the book, I hope you'll connect through the following link so you can know when the next releases will be coming out. Your email address will never be shared, and you can unsubscribe anytime.

www.bookouture.com/lucy-connelly

I love writing the relationship between the twins, but I enjoy the friendships they've made just as much. We all need friends like they have on the court in our lives. People who stand by us and believe in trying to make the world a better place. What do you think about their little gang? What would you like to see more of? I'd love to hear from you. We can connect on social media or through my website.

And as always, thank you for writing those wonderful reviews. It helps authors so much when you tell others how much you enjoyed their books.

Love to you all,

Lucy Connelly

KEEP IN TOUCH WITH LUCY

www.lucyconnelly.com

facebook.com/LucyConnellyBooks

x.com/candacehavens

instagram.com/candace_havens

ACKNOWLEDGMENTS

Many thanks to my editor, Ruth Tross, and the Bookouture team for helping to make this book what it is. And to Maisie Lawrence for helping me come up with the idea. It takes a village to make a novel, and my Bookouture village is amazing.

I couldn't do any of this without my agent, Jill Marsal, who has stood by me in good times and bad. Thank you, Jill, for always having my back.

And thank you, dear readers, for all the love you've shown me and this series. I'm indebted to you all and so very grateful to you for reading the words I write. Thank you also for the reviews and kind words. You have no idea how much your encouragement helps me every day.

PUBLISHING TEAM

Turning a manuscript into a book requires the efforts of many people. The publishing team at Bookouture would like to acknowledge everyone who contributed to this publication.

Audio
Alba Proko
Sinead O'Connor
Melissa Tran

Commercial
Lauren Morrissette
Hannah Richmond
Imogen Allport

Data and analysis
Mark Alder
Mohamed Bussuri

Editorial
Ruth Tross
Imogen Allport

Copyeditor
Jane Eastgate

Proofreader

Anne O'Brien

Marketing

Alex Crow

Melanie Price

Occy Carr

Cíara Rosney

Martyna Młynarska

Operations and distribution

Marina Valles

Stephanie Straub

Joe Morris

Production

Hannah Snetsinger

Mandy Kullar

Jen Shannon

Ria Clare

Publicity

Kim Nash

Noelle Holten

Jess Readett

Sarah Hardy

Rights and contracts

Peta Nightingale

Richard King

Saidah Graham